TICK TOWN

CHRISTOPHER A. MICKLOS

CASTLE BRIDGE MEDIA
DENVER, COLORADO, USA

CASTLE BRIDGE MEDIA
Denver, Colorado

Cover art by Josh Sanabria/Unsplash, Erik Karits/Unsplash, Birmingham Museum Trust/Unsplash. These images have been modified.

TICK TOWN

ISBN: 979-8-9917855-4-9

Praise for Tick Town

"The giant bugs are back with a gruesome vengeance! Lovers of the kind of monstrous plague the Guy N. Smith tradition loosed upon the world should find much to relish in this book."
—RAMSEY CAMPBELL, MASTER OF MODERN HORROR
(*The Hungry Moon*, *The Doll Who Ate His Mother*)

"*Tick Town* is a great throwback to the golden age of pulp horror paperbacks, books like *The Rats*, *Slugs* and *Bats out of Hell*. Books that shaped a genre and gave so much enjoyment to so many. Books like this don't come along very often so make sure you don't miss it."
— SHAUN HUTSON, THE BRITISH GODFATHER OF GORE
(*Slugs*, *Erebus*)

Acknowledgements

WRITING A NOVEL CAN BE a lonely journey, but I've learned from this experience that the road is never truly traveled alone. So some thanks are certainly due.

Thanks to my best pal and first reader Jay Sapiro. He was the only person to lay eyes on TICK TOWN when it was still in its early drafts; and without his enthusiasm and feedback, it might still be just a file on my laptop.

Thanks to my literary agent Mark Falkin, as well as Jason Henderson and In Churl Yo at Castle Bridge Media. They took a chance on a first-time novelist and put up with a lot—and I mean a lot—of questions along the way. I'm grateful for their confidence and trust in the value of my work.

Thanks also to a trio of greathearted, iconic pulp horror authors: the legendary Ramsey Campbell, the superb Graham Masterton, and the great "British Godfather of Gore" Shaun Hutson. When I impetuously reached out to each of them like a drooling fanboy to express my admiration for their work and gratitude for the inspiration they provided me, each one— to my utter astonishment—responded back with generous expressions of encouragement and kind congratulations on my small contribution to the genre. The same can be said for pulp horror great Guy N. Smith's daughter Tara. I reached out to express to her that without her late father's works mine would likely not exist, and she kindly responded back with words of appreciation and support.

And finally, and most essentially, thanks to my extraordinary wife Amanda and my amazing daughter Liv. They are immensely patient and boundlessly supportive of my dreams and ambitions…and I find it simply impossible to summon the words to convey just how much they both mean to me and just how little I would be without them. So I will simply say I'm forever grateful. I'm immensely lucky. And I love you both.

Chapter 1

"OUCH!"

Cheri Butler flinched at the calloused hand rubbing over the pale skin of her flat belly. One month earlier, that skin had boasted a rich, even tan, with two skimpy white patches where her French bikini blocked the sun's rays. Now, three weeks into September, that tan—along with those long summer days at the lake and summer nights around the bonfire—was just a faded memory.

"I barely touched you." Dave Dobbs complained. He leaned down again and pressed his mouth over hers.

His hand cupped her breast over a peach-colored bra. He pressed his tongue into her mouth.

Pushing him off her, Cheri propped herself up on an elbow. She touched the tender area of her exposed skin.

"Wait, get the light."

With a grunt, the twenty-year-old rolled over and retrieved the lantern from across the small tent. He raised the flame while she carefully stroked a finger over a small black spot on her midsection.

"It's just a tick."

"Gross," Cheri pouted.

Dave dug in the pocket of his pea green cargo pants, producing a Zippo lighter with an angry American eagle emblazoned on its face. A sleeve of three Durex condoms tumbled onto the sleeping bag. Cheri glanced at them but was temporarily more concerned with the tick.

"You wanna burn me?" she said, rejecting the lighter. Instead, she reached into her overnight bag and pulled out some tweezers. Wincing, she gingerly dug the tiny parasite out of her skin.

Dave watched her in the lamplight.

Despite the foul procedure, Cheri still cast a lithe, sexy figure in her tight jeans and sheer bra. Her firm nineteen-year-old body was the carnival prize he'd been trying in vain to win since the Fourth of July.

"Oh my God." Cheri finally extracted the disgusting little bloodsucker from its feeding ground in her flesh. Holding it close to the lantern, she made a face. Its eight legs jerked around, struggling to free itself from the pinch of the tweezers.

Cheri passed it to Dave. "Get rid of it."

Dave flipped open the Zippo and ignited it, taking the tweezers and casually moving the tick into the flame. The creature twitched and kicked, fighting to escape the fire. Then its legs curled, and it was just a charred, dead thing.

Tossing the tick and tool away, Dave was immediately on Cheri again. He pushed her down onto her back. She accepted his mouth eagerly.

After several hot moments, Dave broke the kiss. Pressing his luck, he peeled down one cup of her soft bra and let his mouth find her ripe young breast. Cheri gasped, tangled her fingers in his curly blonde hair, and held his teasing mouth against her.

Lost in pleasure, she let herself imagine what it would feel like to give in to Dave, wrap her legs around him, and let him have what he wanted. The thought made her whimper and press her pelvis up against his. He moaned back.

But realizing how close they were to crossing the line, Cheri opened her eyes. She withdrew slightly, pushing her hands gently against his shoulders.

"What do you have those for?"

"What?" Dave was breathless now. He lowered his mouth to her neck.

"What do you have rubbers for?"

Dave stopped trying to kiss her.

"What do you think I have rubbers for?" he growled, suddenly cupping a hand over her crotch. Cheri jerked away.

"Stop it."

"Why?"

"What do you mean *why?*" Cheri scrambled up, adjusting her bra, and reached for her t-shirt. "Just stop."

Dave watched her pull her top back on. His shoulders slumped, "Baby…"

But she wasn't having it.

"You jerk."

"I'm a jerk?" Dave snapped back. "You're a dick tease. You screwed Tommy Carpenter all junior year, and now suddenly you're the Virgin Mary?"

Cheri's face flushed red, her retort catching in her throat. A flood of tears burned her eyes. Without another word, she grabbed her embroidered jean jacket, pushed open the tent flap, and stumbled out into the night.

"Cheri, wait!" Dave called after her. "I'm sorry!"

But it was too late.

He flopped back down onto his back and cursed his own stupidity.

Outside, Cheri tramped along the path through the dense trees. Though just a few miles from town, the darkness and isolation of Tomahawk Woods pressed in on her. Barely enough moonlight filtered through the treetops to keep her on the path.

Cheri scolded herself.

Milly warned you about him, she thought, wondering if it was her cousin who'd told Dave about Tommy. *How could you be so stupid?*

As she stomped along, the fingers of her right hand felt for the delicate bracelet on her left wrist. From the thin chain hung three silver charms—a heart, a lock and key—with three decorative letters elegantly intertwined. A *C*, a *D*, and an *E*.

He gives you a shiny little gift and you fall for it like a dumb little girl!

"Dumb, dumb, dumb," she said aloud this time.

It was several minutes before Cheri paused, not sure what prompted the sudden stop. Growing up in nearby Tomahawk Hollow, these northern Wisconsin woods had been her playground since she was a little girl. It had been more than a decade since anything out here had scared her, even at night. But now something was making her increasingly uncomfortable.

Cheri strained to listen but didn't hear anything. No footsteps rustling the leaves. No low growl of some lurking predator. Nothing. There was no sound at all, apart from her own shallow breathing. And that's what unnerved her. Normally alive at night with the rhythmic chirping of crickets, the scuttling and scurrying of small mammals, and even the occasional call of a hoot owl on high alert, the forest had suddenly gone eerily mute.

Cheri felt the tiny hairs on her arms rise. With chill and dampness all around her, she was suddenly aware of her bare feet. She hadn't pulled her shoes on before exiting the tent. Turning around, Cheri willed her cold feet to start moving again. All she wanted was to get back to Dave and the tent and the comforting light of their campfire.

Imagining malevolent eyes on her, Cheri walked faster, stumbling forward on the path. The anger and regret that had gripped her moments before gave way to a swelling panic. Soon she was running, racing almost blindly along for several long moments before seeing the glimmer of their campfire ahead.

"Dave!" she called out.

Reaching the fire, she stopped, horrified. By the light of the flames she could see a volume of those awful wood ticks covering her bare feet. Certain that she could feel the tiny devils digging into her flesh, Cheri screamed.

Steadying herself, she sobbed "Dave!" again before crawling into the tent through the open flap.

Inside, the lantern had been knocked over, leaving the tent in near darkness. A putrid stench stung Cheri's nostrils. Dave lay on his back, one of their oversized backpacks resting on his chest. His arms and hands splayed out awkwardly to either side of him.

"David Dobbs!" Cheri cried one more time, now as much in anger as in fear. But her boyfriend continued to ignore her.

Cheri reached out a hand to push the backpack off him but drew it back, repulsed. Not the polyester bag she expected, it felt rough and slimy and left her shuddering as she knelt in the tent.

At the same moment, she saw why his hands looked so awkward next to him. Both had been severed from their arms—one at the wrist and the other higher up the forearm—and rested several inches away from the arms they should have been attached to. Blood pooled rapidly over the tent's nylon floor.

In horror, Cheri realized that though Dave hadn't moved, the thing on top of him rose and fell with an eerie, rhythmic pulsation.

Losing command of her senses, Cheri screamed and retreated backwards on her hands and knees, practically crawling right into the fire outside. She gagged and wretched the contents of her stomach onto the grass and then just kneeled there heaving.

Not another second passed before a sharp, searing pain flashed through her left thigh, so intense that she collapsed forward into her own vomit. Before she could push herself up again, something pierced one side of her back and then the other. The agony spread like a kerosene fire through her body until shock overtook her, quickly followed by a rapid descent into total and forever darkness.

Chapter 2

FIFTY-THREE-YEAR-OLD JACKSON Reed sat in a window booth at Gail's Main Street Diner. He slurped lukewarm coffee and watched the activity outside. As owner, publisher, and editor-in-chief of the Tomahawk Hollow Gazette, watching was a professional habit. And there were very few places where you could see or hear more about what was happening in small town Tomahawk Hollow than in a booth by a window in Gail's Main Street Diner.

"Warm it up?"

"Thanks, Tess," Jackson answered as the waitress began to pour.

"Tourists are coming early for the Jubilee this year," she remarked with a nod to the nearly full diner.

"That should make the mayor happy," Jackson noted.

Tess smirked and finished her pour. "Food's out in a minute."

Jackson glanced around the restaurant and began to count the number of diners who held open newspapers in front of them. Another professional habit. It didn't take long, though, as the number of residents who regularly purchased the Gazette had been dwindling for years.

Just as he finished his disappointing count, he spotted Emmaline Blackdeer, his one and only employee, coming through the door. She strode towards him, and Jackson grunted.

"I'm having breakfast, Em…"

But his objection didn't stop her from sliding into the booth across from him and presenting four pages of printed copy. He took it but set it down on the table unread.

"I'll be in the office in an hour," he began, "and since our next edition doesn't come out until Monday, I'm not sure what the rush is."

Converting the Gazette from a daily newspaper to a biweekly had been a painful decision for the veteran newspaperman. But now that they published exclusively on Thursdays and Mondays, he felt he should at least enjoy the fruits of not being on deadline every minute of every day.

"It's for the blog," Emmaline explained, though he surely knew that already.

Emmaline Blackdeer had been working for Jackson for two years. A member of the Bad River Band of Lake Superior Chippewa, she'd grown up on the tribe's reservation, perched on the southern shore of Lake Superior at nearly the northernmost point of northern Wisconsin. Fresh out of community college, she came to the Gazette with a degree in journalism, abundant youthful enthusiasm, and a determination to drag the newspaper into the twenty-first century.

Jackson sighed.

"Emmaline," he used her full name only when a lecture was to follow, "we're a *paid* newspaper. People *pay* for the print edition. People don't pay for that blog I let you talk me into. So, when you post content in a blog that's free, people start to think that they don't need to pay for their news anymore. I'd draw you a diagram, but it would be a *really simple* diagram."

"News doesn't happen twice a week, Jackson. It happens every day, all day."

"Then people should be willing to pay for a daily newspaper," Jackson groused. "But they're not, as we've learned."

"Did you know," Emmaline said, tapping the pages in front of Jackson, "that there's never been a real clean-up job at the old plant?" She was talking about Tomahawk Hollow Pesticides, which had closed its doors three years earlier. "My source says they shut down operations, left town, and the place has been locked up like a drum ever since."

Jackson well knew the history of Tomahawk Hollow Pesticides and the devasting effect its sudden closure had on the town. And he reckoned that Emmaline's "source" was one of the busy-body gossips who worked a few doors down Main Street at City Hall.

"*Tighter than a drum*," Jackson corrected. "You don't lock up a drum."

"My point," Emmaline persisted, "is that they have tanks out there that are still full of dangerous, volatile chemicals, and basically the whole place has just been abandoned."

"And three years later that news can't wait until Monday…why?" Jackson quipped.

"If there was a leak," Emmaline was working herself up, "those chemicals could get into the groundwater. They could drain into Tomahawk River. Heck, the sewer system runs directly from the plant into town!"

Tess returned with a large plate of eggs, pancakes, potatoes, and sausage.

"Here you go," she smiled. "You want anything, Em?"

"Say, Tess," Jackson said, "how about today and tomorrow breakfast is free, and then I'll just pay you for what I eat on Monday'?"

Tess rolled her eyes. "Did you catch that, Em? I think that little parable was for your benefit."

"Nothing for me," Emmaline answered, and Tess was off again.

"Print newspapers enjoyed centuries at the top of the information food chain," she continued. "Newspapers. Books. Magazines. But technology triggers evolution…and evolution is a good thing."

"That's what everyone thinks," Jackson snorted, "until they're not at the top of the food chain anymore."

Even as he said it, though, a ruckus across the diner drew his attention.

Several tables away, an agitated Dan Bulter, Tomahawk Hollow's resident pharmacist, stood over Elmer Dobbs' table. Jackson could see Dan barking at the larger man and poking a finger at his chest. And judging from Elmer's rapidly reddening face, the confrontation was about to escalate. By the time Jackson slipped out of his booth and crossed the diner, Elmer—who had about three inches and ninety pounds on Dan—was out of his chair, glaring down, and clenching his fists.

"Hey, hey, hey," Jackson slipped between the two men. Their dispute had brought the diner to near-silence except for their own raised voices. "What's going on here?"

"Tell this goddamned pill popper to get his finger outta my face," Elmer growled through a clenched jaw, "before I break it off!"

"It's pill *counter*, you buffoon!" Dan retorted. "You're too stupid to even get your insults right!"

"Enough you two!" Jackson snapped. "Danny, what's this about?"

"My daughter wasn't home this morning when I woke up," his voice was trembling, "and Olive tells me that this *animal's* boy dragged her into the woods last night!"

"You snotty lump o' racoon shit. They went campin'." He turned to Jackson. "Like kids do."

"My Cheri doesn't go camping overnight with boys. She's a good girl!"

"A good girl," Elmer snorted, "wouldn't-a spent three months spit-polishin' Tommy Carpenter's ping pong balls last year."

With that both men lunged at each other. Jackson managed to shove them apart.

"Whoa, whoa! Tess, can you call Timmy?"

"Chief's not around this morning, Jackson," Tess told him, hovering just a few steps away. "He had to go out to the Becker farm."

Suddenly, the diner skirmish was all but forgotten as Jackson's news instincts kicked in.

"What's going on at the Becker farm?"

Chapter 3

TOMAHAWK HOLLOW POLICE CHIEF TIM Donovan held one hand over his nose as he crouched in the grass. He'd seen plenty of bad things in his time, but he'd never smelled anything so God-awful.

Kari Becker, who'd been running the farm on her own since her husband ran off last year, had said that this cow and the one laying across the field had both been alive when she wrapped up evening chores yesterday. That meant that they could only have been dead for twelve or thirteen hours at most. Donovan calculated that even thirteen hours wasn't enough time for the kind of rot and decay that might have accounted for such a stink.

"And you haven't touched either of them?" Chief Donovan had confirmed.

"Nope," the farmer had told him before returning to her morning work in the barn.

Now standing alone, Donovan scratched his head. "Where the hell's all the blood?"

The animal had been ripped open, the rupture in its side torn so wide that half of its innards had spilled out onto the ground. Where its ribcage should have been was just a tangled mess of yellow, jagged bones splintered and separated like so many toothpicks snapped into pieces. And judging from the ugly gashes in its jaw, neck, and hind quarters—as well as the trampled grass in a wide diameter around the remains—the doomed beast had not gone quietly.

The scene at the other end of the farm was much the same.

But whatever slaughtered Kari Becker's two cows that night hadn't been the least bit interested in the head, neck, backside, meat, or any of their organs. They were all intact or—at the very least—somewhere nearby. The only thing it had apparently wanted was the blood.

Both beasts were completely desiccated, drained dry of every drop of blood that they had.

"What the hell?"

Startled by the voice, Donovan looked up to see Jackson and Emmaline walking towards him. They gaped at the mangled carcass on the ground.

"Perfect," Donovan grumbled. "How did you find me?"

"You're the only Black guy in town," Jackson quipped. "You're hard to miss."

"I mean how did you know I was out here," Donovan responded, unamused. "This is private property."

"Take it easy, Timmy," Jackson said. "I've known Kari since long before you ever heard of Tomahawk Hollow. Besides, I figured it had to be something important to drag you away during Jubilee week. Does Silas know you're out here?"

Donovan ignored the wisecrack and turned to Emmaline. "Hey, Em."

"What happened?" she answered, all business.

"Kari lost two cows last night, this one and another over there." Donovan waved a finger toward where they found the other remains. "Both in the same shape. Maybe a wolf—"

"A wolf?" Jackson scoffed.

"I don't know," Donovan snapped. "A bear…?"

Emmaline raised the camera hanging around her neck, but Donovan shook his head. "No pictures, Em," he said, stepping between her and the slaughtered cow.

"Are you kidding?"

"We have no idea what happened here. And with tourists flooding in for the Jubilee, I'm not going to put up with a bunch of Bigfoot bullshit or whatever other nonsense people are going to start up with."

"Come on, Tim," she objected. "We don't even publish again until after the festival."

"No way. No pictures. Not stories. No tweets. Nothing. Not until we know what's going on. Mayor's orders."

Emmaline looked to Jackson for support, but he just shrugged. "Mayor's orders."

"We have a right to report this," Emmaline challenged, turning back to the chief. "Ever hear of the First Amendment?"

Donovan fixed her with a look. "Yeah, that's the one about not screwing another guy's wife, right?"

It came out harsher than he'd meant it. Emmaline tightened, face flushing red.

"Look," Donovan continued quickly, "if you wanna take it up with the Supreme Court, be my guest. But no pictures today."

Emmaline bristled—his previous comment still stinging—and then spun on her heels. She strode back towards the driveway and Jackson's car.

"You have yourself a nice day, Em," Donovan called after her.

Jackson just stood there, eyes scanning over the scene.

Chapter 4

THE DAMP BLANKET OF LEAVES squished softly under Henry Wilson's rhythmic footfalls. More accustomed to the paved paths of the River Walk and the Lincoln Park Zoo, he found the woodland trail to be harder work overall but significantly more friendly to his knees. And even for a lifelong Chicagoan, it was hard to beat the brilliant array of colors decorating rural Wisconsin in the early autumn.

The Wilson clan had made the six-hour trek up from the Windy City earlier in the day as a compromise of sorts. Henry had been forced to back out of the family trip to Italy in July due to complications with the Zereny trial. The rest of them had gone on without him, but Marjorie still wanted a full-family getaway. So just two months later they packed the car and headed north for the Harvest Moon Jubilee.

The twins had been near-insufferable the entire drive up, and Maggie hadn't been much better, angry about having to miss the school's freshman dance on Friday. After arriving in Tomahawk Hollow, Henry had them shovel some mediocre diner food into their pie holes for lunch, and then they made their way to the VRBO.

"Isn't it lovely up here?" Marjorie had remarked as they unpacked the car. Henry just stewed and began counting the minutes until they could get back in the car again and head back to civilization.

When Marjorie declared that she and the kids were going to wander around Main Street a bit, Henry decided it was a good time to go for a run. A brochure left for them at the house offered maps of various hiking paths nearby. Henry picked one, made the short drive to the edge of Tomahawk Woods, and then parked and jogged on in.

After twenty minutes, Henry found a nice rhythm and really started to relax. But the intrusive chirp from his pocket brought all the stress right back.

Hell, he thought, *can I not be out of the office for a single day without being bothered?*

His attitude improved dramatically when he saw a text from his secretary, Carly.

How's the family trip?

Henry's lips curled into a grin and he thumbed back a response.

Take a guess. I'm out for a run now to get a few moments peace.

As he waited for Carly's next message, Henry glanced around. A tapestry of sugar maple trees, box elders, and birchwood lined both sides of the path, all in various stages of their journey to their most brilliant autumn colors. Above, their branches and leaves provided an effective canopy against a persistent afternoon drizzle. A few oversized branches had fallen near the path, as had a tree that looked like it had been struck by lightning. One symmetrical oval rock as big as Henry's office desk rested near the tree line. It was strangely discolored or perhaps covered in browning moss.

The phone chirped again.

Oh...so you're alone now?

He raised an eyebrow.

Yes...

How much do you miss me?

His grin widened.

You're bad. What would you do if my wife saw these messages?

The response came back quickly.

I'd tell her shes been replaced.

Henry laughed.

Oh really?

Uh huh. And then I'd show her why.

There was a pause this time as Henry waited for the next text. He stirred just slightly, his imagination churning over what she might be typing or doing.

As he glanced around, though, something suddenly struck him as different. He furrowed his brow, trying to determine what it was, but something about the clearing had changed. He couldn't quite place it. Same trees along the path. Same leaves on the ground. Same fallen branches. But it was like something was missing.

Then he realized.

That strange rock was gone.

But how could that be? Surely he hadn't imagined it?

When Henry's phone chirped again and a picture popped up, the missing rock was the last thing on his mind. Carly sat behind his office desk. The top of the frame cut off her face, with the picture focused on her body as she reclined in his chair. She had removed the jacket that she normally wore, and her crisp white blouse had been unbuttoned completely. It hung open lewdly and exposed her toned twenty-nine-year-old body. A lacy black bra barely contained her firm, round breasts. One hand held the phone, while the other was pushed down under the waistline of her skirt doing God knows what.

Henry's grin returned. He sent another message back.

Take another pic, without the bra.

Almost immediately, Henry's phone began to ring. It was a video call from Carly.

Even better, Henry thought.

He imagined her not only peeling off the bra on camera, but perhaps that skirt, too. His pulse quickened as he wondered what kind of show she had in store for him.

Henry pressed the green button to answer the call.

But before his phone could connect, it fell from his hand, his grip loosened by an abrupt, staggering pain in left leg. Crying out, Henry teetered, suddenly unable to maintain his balance. Toppling over into the dirt and leaves, he crashed down onto his left side without the wherewithal to even break his fall.

Next to him, his phone lay face down on the trail. Carly's muffled voice came from it, "Henry? Where'd you go?"

With excruciating pangs stabbing up through his leg, Henry grasped around desperately for the phone. Before he could reach it, he stopped, eyes bulging in shock. Right next to the phone, he could see his left shoe—his bloody, cleaved-off foot still in it—still standing upright on the path. As he gipped wildly at his leg, blood spewed out from the severed limb and painted the grass and leaves around him.

Movement drew his eye, and Henry realized in near delirium that the rock was next to him now. Four spindly legs protruded from each side of it and carried it towards to him. Even more terrifying, it had a face. What passed for a long, distended mouth twitched, revealing long, fat extensions covered in large, thorny barbs. Henry realized with horror that the wet red streaks splattered over that dreadful mouth was his own blood.

Henry cried out in terror, his mind on the verge of breaking.

The only answer was Carly's concerned voice. "Henry!" she gasped. "Are you alright? I can't see you!"

Despite his desperate attempt to drag himself backwards on his elbows, the monstrous thing was soon on top of him. Henry reached his left hand up to push it away, but a razor-clawed leg slashed towards him. It sliced cleanly through flesh and bone, and the hand went tumbling into the leaves. A gusher of red sprayed from the new wound onto the creature's face—if that's what it really was—and Henry screamed.

"Henry!" Carly's now-panicked voice cried out.

In a stupor, Henry felt his chest open, the splintering of his ribs making a grotesque cracking sound. Then something heavy and thick stabbed into his heart.

The last thing he heard was crying. Sweet, young, sexy Carly, anguished and confused. "Henry! Oh my God, baby, are you okay?" she sobbed as Henry Wilson died alone in the dirt and leaves of Tomahawk Woods.

Chapter 5

"JACKSON!"

The voice called out from across the road as Jackson strode down Main Street in a light afternoon drizzle.

After finishing up at the Becker farm, Jackson had gone back to the Gazette to work on a feature. A couple of local kids would be heading to Madison soon for the state science fair. It was the kind of thing that local readers loved to see in the newspaper.

That story had consumed most of the afternoon, and then he and Emmaline had met for an hour to discuss who would cover what during that weekend's Jubilee. When they were done, Emmaline stayed back at the office to blog about changes to the festival schedule. Jackson headed to the diner and an early dinner.

"Jackson!" the voice persisted, and Jackson finally slowed down. "Jackson Reed! One moment!"

Jackson turned around finally, waiting for his pursuer to catch up with him.

"Mr. Mayor," he greeted without enthusiasm.

Mayor Silas Cankerby was a rotund fellow with chubby legs, squinty eyes, and a perpetual crocodile smile. He was the kind of politician, Jackson always said, who could slap you on the back with one hand and rifle through your pockets with the other.

Still, Jackson gave him credit for keeping the town afloat these last few years. When Tomahawk Hollow Pesticides abruptly closed its doors, it put half the town out of work. Though the abandoned plant still stood there on the edge of town, the tax revenue, jobs, and investments that had once been Tomahawk Hollow's lifeblood were now a distant memory. But just three years later, the mayor had transformed Tomahawk Hollow into a northern Wisconsin tourist destination with a series of special events, celebrations, and festivals. The crown jewel: this weekend's Harvest Moon Jubilee.

"Walk with me, Jackson," the mayor panted.

"What are you doing out?" Jackson teased. "I thought you'd be hunkered down in your office on the phone with the National Weather Service…telling them to turn off the rain."

"I already called," the mayor's grin widened, pleased to be in on the joke. "They said there's nothing they could do about it. But they assured me it'll be sunny and dry by the time the Jubilee kicks off on Friday."

"What can I do for you, Silas?"

They had already reached the entrance to City Hall. The mayor pushed open the door, "Come on inside for a minute."

Jackson suppressed a sigh and followed him into the small suite of cubicles and conference rooms, past the reception desk, and into the big corner office.

Jackson stood in the doorway as the mayor settled in behind his desk. "I don't know where Miriam went, but can I get you a coffee?"

"Yes," Jackson said, calling his bluff, "I'd like you to get me a cup of coffee."

"I'm sure she'll be back soon," the mayor deflected, then got serious. "What were you doing out at the Becker farm this morning?"

"Silas—"

"*Mayor Cankerby*, if you please…"

"*Silas*," Jackson repeated, "I run a newspaper—"

"Oh stop it!" the mayor laughed. "You run a local *business*! So you should be just as focused as I am on the Jubilee this weekend and making sure that all those tourists from all over the state enjoy themselves and keep coming back!"

Jackson let himself sigh this time, but the lecture continued.

"Now, if you need filler for your newspaper, there's going to be plenty happening at the Jubilee! You can run pictures of families enjoying the festival. The Lt. Governor will be here on Saturday. And we'll give you an exclusive interview with the winner of the Miss Harvest Moon pageant."

"Exclusive, huh?" Jackson rolled his eyes. "*The New York Times* will be so jealous."

"What else could you possibly need?"

"Look, Silas, we're not even publishing again until Monday," Jackson said, "so nothing we do will impact your little party. But what happened at the Becker farm is news—"

"*News*," the mayor scoffed. "We live in the wilderness, Jackson! Some…*bear*, or whatever it was…stumbles out of the woods and costs a couple of farmers a few head of cattle. That's not *news*. That's *Wednesday*! I'm not going to let you spark a bunch of silly rumors that impact this festival or anything else we have coming up!"

Jackson stood there for a moment, considering. Then he replied calmly, "I already got the Bigfoot lecture from Timmy, okay? We don't need to go through it again."

"Bigfoot?" Mayor Cankerby sputtered. "What the hell are you talking about?"

"Are we done, Silas?"

The mayor sat behind his desk staring daggers back at Jackson. Then, like Hyde transforming back into Jekyll, his lips curled back into that crocodile smile.

"We're done, Jackson. I'll look forward to reading your coverage of the Jubilee."

Jackson turned, made his way back through the outer office, and exited out to Main Street. By the time he got there, he already had his phone out.

"Hey, Jackson," Emmaline's voice answered.

"Hey." Jackson walked at a brisk pace through the drizzle toward the Gazette. "We need to go talk to your ex-boyfriend first thing tomorrow."

"What's going on?"

"It wasn't just Becker," Jackson said. "Multiple farms got hit. The mayor just confirmed it."

# # #

Back in City Hall, the mayor, too, was making a call. Sitting back at his desk after getting up to close the door, the mayor's chubby fingers punched at the numbers on his office phone. It took six rings before the call picked up.

"What do you want?" a clipped voice asked.

The mayor paused, hesitant to set this wheel in motion.

The voice was impatient, "Hello?"

Finally, the mayor responded.

"I think we have a problem."

Chapter 6

WHEN THEY REACHED THE FIRST fork in the path they'd been following, Elmer Dobbs and Dan Butler stopped. The two men had spoken all of twenty-three words to each other so far that morning. None of them had been particularly gracious. But with exceptions for "idiot" and "pencil dick," they hadn't been overly hostile, either.

Once they had cooled off the day before, Elmer and Dan had found some common ground. Number one, each of them agreed that the other was a terrible parent. Number two, they agreed that their kids were never to see each other again. And finally, they both agreed that once this unpleasant episode was over, if Dan and Elmer ever happened to run into each other again on the street, they'd both turn around and walk the other way.

But then ten o'clock rolled around that night and Dave Dobbs hadn't come home yet. Elmer rang up Dan on the phone and broke their short-lived vow of silence.

"That girl o' yours ever come home? 'Cause my boy sure hasn't."

"Look, you goddamned gorilla…" Dan rejoined, and on it went.

So, first thing Thursday morning, Elmer and Dan begrudgingly drove out to the edge of Tomahawk Woods together. Heading down the main path, they were determined to find their kids and ground them indefinitely.

"Which way?" Dan asked, deferring to Elmer's greater familiarity with the woods.

Elmer didn't answer but kept shuffling on, following the fork to the left.

27

As he followed, Dan took another uneasy glance at the handgun Elmer had resting in the holster at his waist. Dan didn't approve of guns in general. And he certainly wasn't a fan of the idea of trudging through these woods with an armed lunatic.

"What's the gun for?" Dan asked, not for the first time.

"Shootin' things," Elmer responded through a mouthful of chewing tobacco.

"You're funny."

Elmer spat out a cocktail of tobacco juice and saliva, only half of which cleared his chin.

"What'd you bring, a mortar and pesto?" he cackled. He wiped the wet remains off his chin with the back of his hand.

Dan glowered, "It's a *pestle*, you cretin. Mortar and pestle."

"Whatever you say, Martha." Elmer waved a hand dismissively.

Another ten minutes passed in silence, except for the buzz and hum of the forest.

At least the rain stopped, Dan thought, grateful that the persistent morning drizzle seemed to be over. He began to tug off his pullover windbreaker when he stumbled into Elmer, who had inexplicably stopped.

"What the hell?"

"Shut up!" Elmer snapped.

"What?"

"Shut up!" Elmer insisted.

Dan listened for a moment and then heard it.

At first he couldn't make out the sound, but then it became more distinct. Raspy. Inconsistent. Like something struggling to speak or breathe. As the two men stood silently, the faint rasping became more urgent.

Elmer began to follow the sound into the tree line.

"What are you doing?" Dan asked, his voice reduced to an exaggerated whisper.

Elmer ignored him and disappeared into the trees.

With a frustrated grunt, Dan followed.

Stepping over and around fallen branches, rocks, and thick roots rising out of the ground, the two men followed the sound. About one minute from the path—Elmer estimated about twenty yards—they came to a small clearing and saw it.

A good-sized doe lay amongst the leaves. Her breathing was rough and labored. And though she couldn't raise her head from the ground, her frightened eyes tracked their approach.

The closer the two men got, the more they could see.

Fragments of ribs jutted upward out of her exposed chest. The flesh had been shredded and ripped open. Blood was spattered everywhere.

"What happened to it?" Dan wondered aloud.

Elmer just stared. After a moment he shook his head and gave a slight shrug of his shoulders.

Dan persisted, "Can we help it?"

The question snapped Elmer out of his daze. He quickly scanned the edges of the clearing for any signs of another presence nearby. Then, calculating, he took another couple of steps toward the doe and withdrew his handgun from its holster.

"What are you doing?" Dan blurted, though he knew full-well Elmer's intention.

"She's dyin'," Elmer answered. "You don't just let her suffer."

Dan stepped forward this time and put a hand on Elmer's arm, restraining him. "You can't shoot her."

Elmer spat more juice out, just missing Dan.

"This is what men do. If you ain't got the stomach for it, hike up your skirt an' go home."

Next to them, the doe's breathing became quick and even more shallow. The two men redirected their attention back to her, realizing then that she was in her final death rattle. With a slight shutter and one final grunt of misery, the doe went still, her eyes glassy and dull.

Elmer and Dan both looked down at her with pity. Elmer put away his gun.

"That's it," Elmer said. "She gone."

Without another word, Elmer pushed through the trees and headed back toward the trail. Dan followed.

Once they were back on the path, Elmer proceeded back to the route they were following. This time he moved much more quickly.

"Why are you going so fast?"

Elmer ignored him and just strode on, startling his companion with his suddenly grim demeanor and urgency.

Chapter 7

"HOW MANY"?

Only a couple minutes into their conversation, Emmaline had already worked herself into a lather.

She and Jackson had met first thing Thursday so that they could both be waiting for Donovan as soon as he arrived at work. When he saw them standing there, he grimaced, recognizing right away that his day was going to start off on a rotten note.

The Police Station was only two doors over from City Hall. When Donovan had finished up at the Becker farm the previous day, he'd immediately popped over to see the mayor. He'd wanted to update him about the incident at the farm and let him know that the junior sleuths from the Gazette had come poking around. More importantly, he wanted to make it clear that he had shut them down and there wasn't going to be any further inquiry, at least until after the Jubilee. But clearly, Donovan now calculated, Cankerby had gone directly to Jackson and rekindled the whole thing.

"Look—"

"Just answer the question, Tim! We want to know—"

"Don't talk to me that way, Em. I'm in no mood for one of your famous lectures."

"Hey, you ass—"

"Okay, okay!" Jackson intervened, having to this point stayed out of the fray. "Everyone take a breath."

"I'm busy, Jackson," Donovan sighed. "What do you want?"

"How many?" Emmaline repeated.

"How many what?"

Emmaline bristled. Jackson answered.

"Yesterday, you let us believe that the Becker farm was a one-off, but we know for a fact that more farms have been victimized. How many?"

Donovan rubbed his temple, knowing full well he wouldn't be getting rid of them until he gave them something. "This is all off the record," he stipulated.

"Off the record? Where'd you learn—" Emmaline huffed.

But Jackson cut her off again, "Fine. Off the record. How many?"

"Three."

"Three total?" Jackson clarified.

"Three total," Donovan confirmed. "Becker yesterday, and then the Madsens and Lupinskis over the past 48 hours or so before that. Same sort of thing."

"How many animals?"

"Seven total. Cattle, mostly, but one horse. And a few others missing. A fence was wrecked at the Madsen farm, and I figure a couple horses got spooked and ran off."

Emmaline and Jackson glanced at each other, neither of them sure what to make of it.

"What are you thinking, Timmy?" Jackson probed.

"A wolf, maybe."

"Wolves eat animals," Emmaline challenged. "They don't drain their blood."

"Okay, fine," Donovan shrugged. "A vampire, then."

"Come on, Timmy," Jackson said, "just level with us."

"A wolf or a cougar, I think," he answered.

"Yesterday it was a wolf or bear!"

"Well, Em, today it's a wolf or a cougar," Donovan growled, nearing the end of his rope. "Those are the number two and three most dangerous animals you'll find in Wisconsin. So that's my best guess."

"I don't know, Timmy." Jackson wasn't satisfied. "When's the last time someone spotted a cougar up here? Ten years? Twenty?"

"There were sightings in Price and Sawyer Counties last year," Donovan corrected. "It's not unreasonable."

Jackson considered that for a moment. Now that Donovan mentioned it, he did recall having heard something about those sightings the year before. The chief was right, Jackson conceded to himself, it wasn't unreasonable.

Emmaline jumped in again, "Is that it?"

Donovan gave her a tight-lipped smile, "That's it."

"Wolves and cougars leave pretty defined tracks, Timmy," Jackson noted. "As wet as it's been the last twenty-four hours, I imagine there'd be plenty to find in the woods, particularly on the rim near those farms."

"I imagine you're right," the chief agreed.

"Are you going to check it out?" Emmaline pressed.

"Not today. Too much going on in town."

"You're the friggin' Chief of Police—"

"You know, Em," Donovan snapped, "that's kind of an honorary title around here. It goes to the guy who happens to be the only cop in town. So as long as I'm on my own here, I've got to prioritize my time, and right now the Jubilee is my priority."

Emmaline's next objection was cut off by Jackson.

"All this is off the record," Jackson confirmed. "But if we find cougar tracks in the woods, that's going to make for some good photos in the newspaper."

The chief shrugged again, "You do whatever you need to do, Jackson. I'll let you and the mayor fight that out between the two of you."

Jackson nodded and motioned for Emmaline to follow him towards the door, but she didn't move.

"What's number one?" she asked.

"What?"

"You said wolves and cougars were two of the three most dangerous animals up here. What's number one?"

The chief laughed.

"You're barking up the wrong tree. Number one doesn't slaughter livestock. It spreads disease."

Jackson and Emmaline thought for a moment, and then she realized.

"Ticks," she answered.

"Yep," Donovan confirmed. "So if you find a tick in those woods that can tear open a cow, you have my permission to go ahead and print that in the newspaper."

Chapter 8

FORTY-FIVE MINUTES LATER, EMMALINE found herself sitting at a small kitchen table at Jake and Claire Madsen's farmhouse. Claire was pouring coffee as Emmaline fidgeted with her notebook.

After talking with Donovan, Jackson and Emmaline had decided to split up. He wanted to look around Tomahawk Woods to see if he could find any unusual tracks. Emmaline went to talk with the other farmers who had lost livestock that week. She started at the Lupinski farm, but they had waved her off. They were too busy with their morning chores to speak with her, they claimed. So she aimed her car in the direction of the Madsen farm to see if they'd talk with her.

On the short drive between the farms, Emmaline's eyes were drawn to the old Tomahawk Hollow Pesticides plant in the distance. It sat perched on the edge of Tomahawk Woods just beyond the fields, and it was visible from each farm she visited.

Emmaline had moved to Tomahawk Hollow a full year after the plant closed, so she had never actually been inside. But she and Tim had taken a walk out there last spring, just outside the tall fence that kept tourists away from the plant. She remembered being surprised at how big it was. She had suggested to him that they sneak in and look around, but Tim—who was new to Tomahawk Hollow himself—said the fence was there for a reason. And when he began to brush soft kisses over the back of her neck, she decided that they had much better things to do with their lazy afternoon.

Emmaline sipped at the black coffee that Claire Madsen had poured her and made a face. She glanced over to make sure that Claire hadn't noticed and was relieved to see that she hadn't, still busying herself at the stove.

"Tim says it was a wolf or bobcat that killed your livestock," Emmaline said.

Claire remained with her back to Emmaline. "That's what he said."

"Do you have any reason not to believe him?"

The question drew Claire's attention. She craned her head around to look at Emmaline.

"No, why would I?"

"No reason," Emmaline answered, trying to affect a casual tone. "Just curious if you or your husband thought otherwise."

Claire eyed her for a moment and then turned her attention back to the stove.

"You and Chief Donovan were quite an item there for a while, weren't you?" Claire asked, this time affecting a casual nonchalance herself.

"Excuse me?"

"Engaged, weren't you?"

"We dated," Emmaline corrected, her cheeks flushing. "We weren't engaged."

"What happened?" Claire asked with just a hint of a smirk. "You seemed like such a good match. Both being—" she fumbled for just a moment to find a good substitute for the word she was originally going to say, "—*outsiders*, and all."

"Well, you know…" Emmaline began to stammer, but Claire had already moved on. She sat down at the table with Emmaline.

"Anyway," Claire said, "if the chief says that's what it was, then I'm sure that's what it was. We just hope it doesn't come back."

Emmaline took another sip of that bitter coffee. This time she forced a thin smile as she swallowed. Claire seemed pleased.

"Can I see the animals?" Emmaline asked. "Just to get some pictures."

"Whatever for?"

"The paper."

Claire wrinkled her face.

"I think that's what they call 'sensationalism', isn't it?" she noted disapprovingly.

Emmaline sipped again, "People will be interested."

"Well," Claire shook her head, "I guess you know better than I do. But they already took them away."

Emmaline perked up. "Who did?"

"DNR men, I suppose," Claire answered. "They were here early this morning."

It seemed odd to Emmaline that the State Department of Natural Resources would have moved so quickly. Between the standard bureaucracy and so many budget cuts in recent years, resources and personnel were spread awfully thin.

"That's strange, don't you think?"

Claire just shrugged, "We're just glad to get them out of here."

Emmaline paused and then registered what Claire had said the moment before.

"Why did you say you 'suppose"?

"What?"

"You said 'DNR men, I suppose'."

"Oh, I don't know," Claire laughed. "That's what they said. They just seemed dressed a little strange for DNR men."

"Strange?"

"You know, just a little nicer. Cleaner, maybe. Their clothes. More *ironed*." Claire laughed again. "Maybe that's just how they are nowadays."

Emmaline nodded slowly, "Anything else?"

Claire thought for a moment. "Well, the one talked a little funny, so I guess that was odd, too."

"Funny how?" Emmaline asked. "Like an accent?"

"No, not really," Claire considered. "You know how like in that movie this summer with that English actress, what's her name? Playing an American. But you know she's a foreigner? Like that."

"You think he was from England?"

"No," Claire corrected. "Just different...but trying not to sound like it."

Chapter 9

JACKSON PULLED HIS CAR INTO Lot 3, located at the northeastern entrance to Tomahawk Woods, and parked.

There was only one other vehicle in the lot, which wasn't terribly unusual mid-week. It was a BMW Series 5 sedan. Jackson peeked inside through the driver's window, noting the all-leather interior, the seat-heater controls, and the high-end radar detector. He didn't need to see the Illinois plates to know this was a tourist's car.

Walking back to his own less lavish Corolla, Jackson popped the trunk. He reached in and retrieved his Remington Model 7.

More than a decade had passed since Jackson had been deer hunting, but he still kept the classic rifle in the back of a closet with a few boxes of ammunition. And though there hadn't been an animal attack on an actual person in years around here, the image of that livestock torn apart motivated Jackson to break the rifle out of storage.

With the gun slung over his shoulder and his refurbished Canon Rebel camera around his neck, Jackson made his way into the woods.

Despite what Jackson had said to Donovan earlier, the floor of the forest had already dried out substantially. Making out tracks of any kind on the dirt path was harder than he thought it would be. And, despite his bravado, Jackson wasn't exactly an expert tracker. Fox tracks could look pretty similar to wolf tracks, as he recalled. And beyond size, he wasn't sure he'd be able to distinguish one from the other.

In fact, he hadn't actually seen wolf tracks in more than thirty years. He had vivid memories of his dad taking him out into those woods as a kid on a wet Sunday, pointing out different tracks as they walked along the trail. His father loved the outdoors and was an avid hunter. Jackson himself could take or leave hunting, but he went out with his dad enough to eventually become a decent shot.

Stopping suddenly on the path, Jackson realized that he'd lost himself in thoughts of his father and stopped paying close attention to the path. How long had he been walking, he wondered? A half hour? Forty-five minutes? He quietly cursed himself for losing his focus.

Deeper in the woods now, Jackson noted that the paths here were still a bit damp, more protected from the drying sun by the thick foliage overhead. Glancing around at the ground, he laughed out loud. It appeared that he'd stumbled across exactly what he was looking for.

"I'll be damned," Jackson muttered, crouching down to get a better look.

Sure enough, there at his feet was a distinct footprint that could only have been made by a wolf. And a big one, too. He was surprised at how easy it was to recognize. Five indentations pressed into the dirt, the heal-pad and four tear-shaped toes that curved into sharp points. The width of the thing was somewhere between five-to-six inches, easily bigger than any wolf print Jackson had ever seen before. He extrapolated the size of the beast from the size of the print and blew a low whistle.

Without thinking about it, he felt for his Remington to assure himself that it was still hanging there.

Gathering himself, Jackson fidgeted with his Canon, focusing on the print and snapping several pictures from various angles. For scale he placed his left hand down onto the path next to the print and shot a few more pictures, unnerved to see that the paw must have been bigger than his own hand.

Jackson was not a small man, standing just a hair more than six feet tall. In high school, he had played power forward for Tomahawk Hollow's Division 3 state champion basketball team. And though the years had softened his muscles and stolen his youthful athleticism, he remained healthy and imposing for a man his age.

But this wolf, he figured, was probably even bigger than him.

Standing up and looking further around the path, Jackson was able to make out two more tracks along a straight line leading into the trees. Based on the size and position, he determined that it was just one wolf making all the tracks. From their depth and general appearance, he calculated that they must have been made when the ground was even wetter than it was now. Several hours at least.

Still, Jackson's curiosity tugged him toward the trees.

Hanging the Canon back around his neck, Jackson stepped slowly and cautiously off the path. He scanned the ground as he went for more tracks. Twenty yards into the trees, he still hadn't found any, but he worked to maintain as straight a line as he could. For another ten yards or so he pressed on, but he halted when he smelled something vaguely familiar. Rancid and corrupt, but familiar. He sniffed at the air, and the stink sent a shudder rippling over him. It was the same thing he'd smelled at the Becker farm the day before.

Something about that smell and what he'd seen the last time he smelled it raised the hairs on the back of his neck. Jackson unslung the rifle from his shoulder. Having the Remington in his hands made him feel better.

Pushing through some overgrown foliage with the butt of the rifle, Jackson pressed forward. With each step he took, the stench got stronger.

And then he saw the wolf.

Jackson gasped at the sight, the thumping in his chest getting harder and faster. He pushed aside some branches to get a better look and knew immediately that they had been wrong.

Whatever it was that killed those livestock back in town had gotten the wolf, too.

Laying in a mass of blood-stained dirt and leaves, the wolf must once have been bigger than any Jackson had ever seen before. In life, it indeed would have been bigger than Jackson and weighed at least two-hundred and forty pounds. But now it was diminished. Broken, gutted, and emaciated like the slaughtered livestock at the Becker farm. And, like that gruesome scene the day before, there was blood splattered in all directions. But not nearly as much as there should have been.

Just beyond the dead wolf, Jackson noticed something else. A sizeable section of the foliage had been slashed away, creating a makeshift path. It was as if someone had hacked their way through with a machete. But the path wasn't tall enough for a man to pass through, rising only as high as his chest, at the most.

Nervously, Jackson gripped the Remington tighter and snapped the bolt to chamber a round of ammunition.

Then, making his decision, he moved forward.

Following the crude path, he pushed aside the higher branches and growth to make enough room for him to pass. It wasn't long before he came to another clearing, and upon stepping into it, he stopped again. There was no more path carved out along its borders, and nothing but a large mass positioned in the middle of it.

At first Jackson thought the mass was a rock. Its general shape and color gave that impression. But then Jackson felt his blood go cold, and his grip on the Remington became damp and clammy.

That rock.

That oddly symmetrical oval rock.

It was *looking* at him.

Mouth hanging open as the rock rose, Jackson saw the thing suddenly reveal four pairs of curled legs underneath it. It stood, lifted what passed for its head, and Jackson found himself staring into the face of a monster.

And though he gaped in disbelief, he immediately recognized what it was.

Jackson was staring at a giant tick.

Tens of thousands of times bigger than any tick he'd ever imagined could exist, its body was three feet across. Its long, strange head sprouted an array of fearsome mouthparts that looked to Jackson like they could casually gut him or rip him to shreds.

Long, thin legs carried it forward. In what seemed almost slow motion, one of the front legs reached out toward Jackson. The end of it curled into a deadly, scythe-like claw that snaked forward with creeping deliberation.

Then, with a sudden alacrity, it slashed toward Jackson's lower leg, and he stumbled backward just quick enough to avoid losing a foot.

Hands trembling, Jackson raised the Remington and fired. The blast slammed into a hard protective shell covering the front of the creature's body. Shards of the natural armor exploded off the creature, but the bullet didn't penetrate it. Stunned but not hurt, the tick faltered back two steps and wobbled just slightly on those long legs. Then its entire frame quaked with a sudden outburst of bestial rage.

And then it advanced again.

Jackson couldn't believe that the nearly point-blank shot had failed to stop the monster.

Fumbling with the bolt, he chambered a second round and fired again. Pieces of tick flew into the air once more and paused its advance, but still no real damage was done.

Seeing those clawed front legs waving towards him and its fearsome mouth twitching excitedly, panic gripped Jackson. But with the creature about on top of him, he managed to gather his wits and spot a vulnerability.

Jackson leveled the Remington, focused, and squeezed the trigger.

With the barrel of the weapon just a few feet from its target, the shot found its mark. The tick's left eye ruptured in an explosion of ropy yellow goo that splattered over its chipped carapace.

The tick expelled a piercing shriek that stung Jackson's eardrums. It wobbled backwards and lurched from side to side in furious pain. Having never known distress, the tick seemed to freeze, unsure of whether to advance or retreat.

Seizing the opportunity, Jackson raised the gun again, snapping the bolt and chambering round four of four. This time, he meant to aim for the other eye. But with the two optic organs positioned to the sides of the monster's head, he couldn't draw a bead. Instead, he zeroed in on the spot that had already proved vulnerable and steadied himself.

Last round, Jackson thought, *and that thing isn't going to sit there while I reload.*

Jackson fired, and the tick screeched again as a second bullet followed the first into its left ocular cavity. Again, yellow goop splattered out—less this time—and again the horrible tick tottered backwards.

This time Jackson didn't wait.

Turning, he plunged back into the trees, sprinting back the way he'd come. Brush and branches tore at his face and arms, resisting his retreat. But Jackson was a man possessed. Only once did he look back, half-expecting to see the tick pursuing him and about to strike. But it was nowhere to be seen. Jackson focused forward, passing the huge dead wolf and forcing his way through the tangled foliage until he was back on the main path.

Gulping air, Jackson allowed himself only a moment of rest. He caught his breath and then took off back down the path, eager to escape Tomahawk Woods and the monster it harbored.

Chapter 10

THERE WAS NOTHING UNUSUAL ABOUT a stranger checking in at the Main Street Inn. It happened year-round; and especially during events like the Harvest Moon Jubilee, strangers were everywhere. But Karl Kellerman definitely put the *strange* in *stranger*.

Standing three inches past six feet tall, Kellerman was built solid but lanky. His long arms reached abnormally far past his waist as he stood perfectly upright and board-stiff, his palms pressed flat against the sides of his thighs. Greasy jet-black hair—a dye job if ever there was one—contrasted unnervingly with his sickly pallid complexion. And drooping over his crisp white button-down shirt was a black suit at least two sizes too big for him. Dark black sunglasses covered his eyes.

Standing at the front desk, he drew uneasy stares from the tourists and staff. He either had no idea how out-of-place he looked or simply didn't care.

Across the lobby, Chief Donovan couldn't help but notice the odd presence standing at the front desk. During the days leading up to the festival, he made a point of checking in frequently with local businesses, particularly the ones catering to the tourist crowd. In the case of the Main Street Inn, Donovan would stop by at least three times a day until the festival was finished.

Now, crouching low to pet the dog of an elderly woman from Iowa who he'd been chatting with, Donovan fixated on Kellerman.

Though generally careful not to profile—Donovan himself had been pulled over more than once for driving while black—he was also a big believer in the tried-and-true law enforcement principle of "where there's smoke, there's fire." And it seemed unlikely that this guy was in town for the Harvest Moon Jubilee.

Standing up, he excused himself from his conversation and walked across the lobby toward the stranger. Before he could reach the front desk, though, his cell phone rattled with a text message from Mayor Cankerby.

Get your butt back to your office!

Donovan read the message, annoyed and ready to ignore it.

Then the phone rattled again with an immediate follow-up.

NOW!!!!

Cursing the mayor under his breath, Donovan pocketed the phone, making a mental note to check back in with the hotel staff later. Then he turned and made his way back out onto Main Street.

"Alright then, Mr. Smith," the young assistant manager said, using the name that was on both the reservation and his credit card. "Here's your key, and if there's anything at all we can do to make your stay more pleasant, please let us know."

Kellerman stood stone still, eyes masked by those dark lenses. He heard her voice but didn't respond. His eyes focused intently on the large silver vase just behind her head. In it, he had been watching the reflection of the dark-skinned man in the police uniform approaching him from behind. Only when the man stopped, turned, and left the inn did Kellerman return his attention to the business at hand.

"Mr. Smith?"

"Thank you," his words came out awkwardly, as if he were making an effort to elongate the "a" as he took the key.

Plucking up two large aluminum suitcases resting near his feet, Kellerman turned and made for the curving staircase up to the second floor. The crowd of people in the lobby parted for him like the waters of the Red Sea.

Go ahead and look, Kellerman thought, *but just pray to your God that I never have cause to look at you.*

After locking and bolting the door to his second-floor room, Kellerman placed one of the two suitcases under the small bed in the middle of the room and slid it far enough back to render it undetectable. Next, he placed the other metal suitcase on top of the bed and opened it. One by one he removed and checked the various weapons and equipment sitting snugly in the various foam compartments. After examining each item, he secured them back into place.

Kellerman had arrived in Tomahawk Hollow several hours ago. The call from corporate headquarters last night had interrupted his short leave at his brother's ranch in Southern Florida, and within two hours he had assembled his team. Their private flight took off from Miami Opa Locka Airport at 5:00 a.m., and they were on the ground in Eagle River, Wisconsin, two hours later.

Kellerman looked around at the tiny rural airport with its two asphalt runways and scowled. *Where on God's earth have they sent us?*

The six-man team divided themselves between the two waiting black vans—four men into the passenger van and the other two into the cargo van—and began the ninety-minute drive to Tomahawk Hollow.

As they drove, Kellerman scanned the environment.

He was certainly familiar with Tomahawk Hollow, having sat in on several crisis management meetings some years back. But he had never actually put boots on the ground. Now, drawing nearer to their destination, he was pleased to note how isolated the town was from other communities, confirming his mission research. That would certainly be helpful if dramatic containment efforts were required.

Once they arrived in Tomahawk Hollow, they proceeded to visit the three farms that had been identified as having reported incidents. None of the farmers they met were particularly concerned about who these strange men were or where they came from, so long as they hauled away the slaughtered carcasses. Particularly when the men provided generous cash payments to reimburse the farmers for their lost livestock. It was something that the Wisconsin DNR had never done before, as far as any of them knew. It was also something that Claire Madsen would fail to mention to Emmaline later that day.

After they finished at the third farm, Kellerman dispatched two of the team members to dispose of the remains. He and the other three then made their way to the rental home on the outskirts of town that would serve as their field headquarters. There they unloaded the crates of weapons, secure communications gear, and other equipment that they had transferred from the plane.

Kellerman then dispatched his three underlings to their post on the outskirts of the town. They were under strict orders to secure the site but to not enter. Their orders were extremely clear about that.

Kellerman then made his way to his downtown hotel.

In the event that he would be ordered to initiate Omega Protocol, he would need a centralized location. The Main Street Inn was smack-dab in the center of the town proper. In addition, the hotel provided immediate access to the mayor and the Chief of Police, whose offices were downtown and who would—he was assured—be helpful local assets during this operation.

Now in his hotel room, equipment all checked and put back away, Kellerman remained perched on the bed and turned on the television set. Just a couple clicks of the remote and he found a mindless American game show, which he watched, expressionless.

Chapter 11

CHIEF DONOVAN LIT HIS CIGARETTE, drew a long drag, and let that first hit of nicotine jolt his system. He'd given up smoking when he was with Emmaline. Not for her, he insisted, but because it was a filthy habit. But he reserved the right to fall off the wagon from time to time, and this was one of those times.

The mayor fanned a hand in front of his own face to keep the smoke away. "Must you, Tim," he complained. "I thought smoking was particularly bad for you people."

Donovan sat behind his desk in the police station, while Mayor Cankerby and Jackson sat in the two chairs across from him. Emmaline hovered near the closed door.

"By 'you people' you mean cops, I assume?" Donovan answered.

"I know, I know," Cankerby chuckled, "I'm just an ignorant small-town racist, right? My apologies for worrying about your health."

Jackson was on the verge of boiling over. He had told them all the story of his encounter in Tomahawk Woods, and nobody had believed him. Even Emmaline seemed dubious.

"What are you going to do about that thing in the woods?" Jackson snapped.

Sighing, the mayor shook his head and then fixed Donovan with a piercing look, putting the ball firmly in his court. The chief scowled back but complied.

"Look, Jackson, something obviously happened to you out there…" he said, indicating the cuts and bruises on the newspaper publisher's face and arms. "But what you're saying is…implausible."

Jackson, who was a professionally trained skeptic, understood their doubts. But he saw what he saw. He directed his answer to the mayor, knowing full well who was in charge, even in the chief's office.

"Why the hell would I make something like this up?"

"Jackson, just calm down," the mayor responded, working hard to maintain his own cool. "Nobody thinks you're making it up. We just think you're—"

"Crazy?" Jackson interrupted.

"*Mistaken*," Mayor Cankerby corrected. "Like Tim said, *something* happened to you, that's clear. But in the heat of the moment, your mind was obviously playing ticks on you."

Donovan snorted in spite of himself, and the mayor broke into a broad, self-congratulatory smile.

Jackson, however, was not amused. "Oh, that's funny."

Emmaline leapt to Jackson's defense, "Do you think this is a joke?"

"Em, take it easy," Donovan admonished.

"Don't talk to me like I'm a little girl," she fumed.

"Then don't act like one."

"Enough, now!" the mayor huffed, determined to restore order to proceedings. "And you mind your tone, missy," he warned. "I don't even know why you're here."

"She's here," Jackson intervened, "exactly because of this kind of nonsense. A little wink here…a little joke there…and the whole thing gets swept under the rug."

"Don't be so dramatic, Jackson," Mayor Cankerby said. "This is not some big, complicated thing." He pointed to Jackson's camera. "You saw wolf tracks in the mud and you took pictures. Fine, we saw them with our own eyes. Big fella, too. Clearly—and I mean *clearly*—the animal that came out of the woods and killed all that livestock. Just like Tim told you yesterday."

"Silas—" Jackson tried to interrupt, but the mayor wasn't finished.

"Then you follow the tracks and find what?" he continued. "A wolf! A big wolf lying dead in the woods. And that's a problem? Heck no! That's the solution. No more wolf, no more problem."

"Except there was a giant goddamned tick the size of this desk that killed the wolf," Jackson exclaimed. "New problem!"

"And did you get a picture of *that*, Jackson?" the mayor pressed. "Can we see *that* picture?"

They all glared at each other. This was getting them nowhere.

After a few moments, Donovan broke the silence.

"Where are you on this, Em?"

"What?"

"Do you believe he saw a giant tick in the woods?"

Emmaline bristled at being put on the spot. The idea of a massive insect stalking Tomahawk Woods was thoroughly unbelievable, but she certainly didn't want to side with Donovan and the mayor.

"I believe Jackson," she finally said.

Donovan pressed, "You believe there's a giant tick roaming the woods?"

"I *believe*," she continued, choosing her words carefully, "that that's what Jackson believes he saw."

Jackson threw her a sharp look, and the mayor jumped in again.

"Exactly! We all agree: Jackson *believes* that's what he saw. But clearly, that's not what it was."

Shaking his head, Jackson sighed in frustration. "Silas, how long have we known each other? Do you really think I'm so addle-brained that I can't tell the difference between a giant tick and a bobcat or a bear…or whatever it is you want me to believe it was?"

"I think," this time it was the mayor choosing his words carefully, "that you want to believe that there's a giant tick in those woods." He paused. "That kind of story would sure sell a lot of newspapers, wouldn't it?"

Once again, Jackson's back was up. "Oh for God's sake, Silas—"

"Jackson," the mayor boomed, raising his voice for the first time, "your newspaper is limping from one money-losing quarter to the next. You're personally buried in so much debt that I can't imagine how you're ever going to get out of it. And if I woke up one morning and told the City Treasurer to call in your overdue property taxes, you'd be out of business by lunch!" The last part seemed less a statement of fact than a direct threat. "So, yes, do I think you're willing to believe some cockamamy story that'll boost circulation and get you a couple days of notoriety? Damn right I do!"

The mayor's words hung in the room for several long moments as everyone stood glaring at each other.

Jackson was at a loss.

"Look, Jackson," Donovan began diplomatically, his cigarette down to the butt by now. "Whatever it was you saw out there killed the wolf, right? So that's done. And *whatever* it was—" Donovan parsed the sentence so that each of them could decide for themselves what "whatever" meant. "—you shot it twice in the eye, right?" He locked eyes with Jackson. "Right?"

"Yes."

"Okay, then," Donovan continued, as if the issue had been resolved. "So it's dead. You're not going to shoot anything point blank in the eye and it's not gonna die. Much less twice. So, thank you. We appreciate you taking care of that."

Jackson scowled, understanding fully that this was the end of it as far as the local authorities were concerned. He stood and walked over to Emmaline at the door.

"You're welcome," he answered sarcastically. "But if that thing isn't dead, we still have a hell of a problem out there that we're going to have to do something about. God forbid it decides to attend the Jubilee."

The mayor's broad smile had returned. "You let us worry about that, Jackson. And you just enjoy the festivities."

Emmaline and Jackson exchanged glances and then were halfway out the door before the mayor's voice stopped them once more.

"And Jackson," he grinned. "If I see anything even remotely irresponsible in that little paper of yours, just remember that the City Treasurer's office is right next to mine."

Neither Jackson nor Emmaline responded, closing the door behind them with a bang.

When they were gone, Donovan crushed out his cigarette on a soft drink can.

"You're not very subtle, are you?"

Mayor Cankerby sniffed and shook his head, standing up himself. "Relax, Tim. You said it yourself. It's over. The thing is dead."

"What thing? The *bobcat*?" He emphasized the last word derisively.

#   #   #

Jackson stomped down Main Street toward the Gazette offices with Emmaline a step and a half behind him. He hadn't known what to expect when made his way directly from his harrowing encounter in Tomahawk Woods to the Police Station, but it certainly wasn't that.

"You didn't really help me out back there, did you?" he said without glancing back at Emmaline.

"I'm not sure what you wanted me to say, Jackson," Emmaline sputtered.

"Do you trust him?"

"What?"

"I know you two have your issues," Jackson said, "but do you trust Tim?"

"Jackson, I don't know what you mean—"

"Look," Jackson said, "I sit in on city budget hearings, and I know there's money allocated every year for a couple of deputies. But Timmy never uses it. He lets those positions sit vacant. Don't get me wrong, this isn't a race thing, but it always seemed suspicious to me that a cop wouldn't want any other cops in town."

"It's not like that," Emmaline said, uncomfortable with the conversation.

They arrived at the Gazette and let themselves in.

"So what's it like?"

"Look," Emmaline began hesitantly, "he doesn't talk about this—he barely told me when we were together—but he had some trouble when he was working in the city."

"What kind of trouble?"

Emmaline pursed her lips and let out a long breath.

"Tim's first job out of the academy was working down in Milwaukee," Emmaline began. "And not the Third Ward. I'm talking about some rough neighborhoods. There were lots of older cops with their own ideas of how to do things. Not bad cops, I guess, but jaded. Cynical. I don't know. Definitely set in their own ways. Tim was different, and it didn't always sit well with the other members of his department. As a result, he became pretty isolated. His partner was rarely around, and the other cops were not exactly quick to support him."

"Well, one day," Emmaline continued, "Tim takes a call about a domestic disturbance, and when he gets there and surveils the situation, it turns out there's a lot more going on. There's some really bad characters there and a drug deal is going down, so—just as he's supposed to—Tim calls for backup. Well, right after he does, the situation escalates, and they begin to assault a young girl who's caught in the middle of it all."

"By 'assault' you mean…?"

"Yeah, that's what I mean," Emmaline confirmed. "So, at that point, Tim can't keep waiting. He enters the premises, engages with the bad guys, but he's outnumbered and the whole thing goes upside down. The girl managed to run off, but Tim was overpowered, beaten bloody, and basically left for dead." Emmaline paused. "His backup never came."

"Jesus," Jackson breathed.

"So," she continued, "after a month in the hospital, he quit his job and came up here. He says he'd rather be the only cop in town and know that he's on his own than call for backup again and be left hanging out to dry."

"Wow," Jackson said, "I didn't know any of that." Then, carefully, he continued, "I guess that makes him particularly sensitive about being betrayed."

Emmaline stared back at Jackson, heat rising in her chest.

"Betrayed?" she repeated through tight lips.

"Never mind that now, we have work to do," Jackson said, ushering Emmaline into her desk chair and motioned to her laptop. "We need to start by finding someone who knows a lot about ticks."

Emmaline bristled but started clicking at her keyboard.

Chapter 12

"CAN I GET YOU ANYTHING else?"

Donovan looked up at Tess, but with a mouthful of meatloaf, he couldn't respond verbally. Instead, he shook his head and Tess was gone, moving on to another table in the packed diner.

Things in town always started to get busy on the Wednesday night before the Jubilee's Friday kick-off. Tourists would arrive in town ahead of the festival for canoeing on the river, hiking in the woods, and enjoying the region's many outdoor attractions before the weather began to turn. In two more weeks, the first hints of winter chill would hit northern Wisconsin, along with more rain and sometimes even some October snow.

"Chief?"

Donovan looked up to see an unfamiliar face standing over him.

"I'm Chief Donovan," he confirmed after swallowing.

"My name is Marjorie Wilson," she said, surprising Donovan by sliding into the booth across from him. "I came by the police station earlier today, but there was nobody there."

"I'm sorry, Miss…"

"Wilson."

"…Wilson. We've been pretty busy around here, so I'm stretched a bit—"

"My husband is missing," she interrupted.

Donovan put down his fork and leaned forward more attentively. "I'm sorry. Please go on."

"We arrived in town yesterday from Chicago," Marjorie said. "My husband, my kids, and me." She flicked her eyes back across the diner, and Donovan noted a booth with three kids nudging and pushing at each other as they gobbled their dinners. "And then the kids and I went out, and when we got back to the rental house he was gone."

"I see. Have you tried calling him?"

"Of course I've tried calling him," Marjorie snapped. "It goes to voicemail. After I tried your office this morning, I called the sheriff's office, but they said I had to wait twenty-four hours."

Donovan tried not to react, but inside he fumed. Sheriff Buckley had made it clear more than once that he didn't think much of Tomahawk Hollow, particularly after the town narrowly voted for his challenger in each of the last two elections. And though his home base in Antigo was only about twenty miles away, it might as well have been in Canada for how often he or his deputies showed their faces in town.

"Well, technically, there's no time limit on when you can file a missing persons," Donovan explained, "but people usually do turn up within twenty-four hours with a pretty reasonable explanation, so…"

"Well, *technically*," Marjorie pressed, "it's now been *more* than twenty-four hours, so I'd like you to take it seriously."

Chief Donovan paused, processing what she was saying.

"Look, Miss…"

"*Wilson*," she repeated again, this time impatiently. "*Mrs.* Wilson."

"*Mrs. Wilson*, I'm sorry. Do you have any idea where he might be?"

"No."

"Or who he might be with?"

Marjorie gritted her teeth, "No."

"Any suggestions at all on where we'd start?"

"No."

Recognizing that she was holding something back, Donovan fixed her with a penetrating look. "Ma'am, you want me to take this seriously, and I will. But you need to, as well."

Swallowing hard, Marjorie answered reluctantly. "Yesterday evening and a couple times today, his secretary called my phone looking for him."

"Is that unusual?"

"Very," Marjorie conceded, clipped and uncomfortable.

Donovan waited for her to say more, but she didn't.

"Look, Mrs. Wilson—"

"Normally when I don't know where my husband is," Marjorie blurted out, "Carly does. And she doesn't exactly call to tell me about it. Do you understand?"

Donovan eyed her closely and nodded, "Yes, I understand."

Chief Donovan wiped his mouth with his napkin and stood. Marjorie stood, too, not sure what was happening.

"Let's go over to my office," he said, counting out a handful of bills to toss onto the table, "and we can at least get some paperwork going and get a bulletin out to other law enforcement in the region. Okay?"

"Thank you."

"And Mrs. Wilson," Donovan continued, "I'm going to need his secretary's phone number."

#   #   #

Elmer Dobbs pulled his well-used Ford truck into the driveway of Dan Butler's two-story home. The Butlers lived just a block off Main Street and within walking distance of the Butler Family Pharmacy. Elmer shifted the vehicle into park. "I'll pick you up at seven tomorrow." It was not a request or a suggestion.

Dan looked over at him. Ever since they had found that deer, Elmer's demeanor had shifted from angry to anxious. But even though Elmer had lived in Tomahawk Hollow much longer than the Butlers had, Dan had lived there long enough to know that those weren't dangerous woods. He couldn't figure why Elmer was so uneasy. As far as Dan was concerned, his daughter was in much more danger from Elmer's son than from anything else out there. Still, he agreed that they should continue looking for them tomorrow.

By the time Dan got to his front door, Elmer had already driven away.

Dan let himself in and found Olive Butler waiting for him at a small table in their living room.

"Anything?" she asked, fidgeting with a puzzle.

Dan kissed his wife and sat down across from her.

"No, but those are big woods," he conceded. "There's a lot of ground to cover."

Olive shook her head and *tsk*'d. "I tried her cell a few times to warn her that you two barbarians were on the warpath, but it kept going to voicemail. Probably has her phone off. I don't blame her."

"We're going back out in the morning."

"Oh, Dan," Olive frowned, "just let them be. They're both over eighteen, and it's not like she didn't tell us where she was going!"

Dan fixed her with a look.

"The more time I spend with that animal," Dan said, "the more convinced I am that we need to keep our Cheri away from that juvenile delinquent son of his."

"Stop it. Davey's a good boy," Olive soothed. "He's just rough around the edges. That's what happens when you lose your mother that young."

"What are you talking about?"

"Clara Dobbs! She passed away twelve or thirteen years ago. Long before we ever came to town. I told you that."

"I guess I didn't remember," Dan confessed.

"So be kind. It couldn't have been easy on that man, losing his wife and raising that boy all on his own."

For just a moment, Dan imagined what it would be like without Olive, but just the thought of it brought such an ache that he pushed it away as quickly as he could. Instead, he just repeated, "We're going back out in the morning."

Olive sighed and shook her head, standing up.

"Come on," she kissed his forehead and started off toward the kitchen. "I'll warm you up some dinner."

Chapter 13

"THANK YOU AGAIN FOR TALKING to us on such short notice," Jackson said. He squeezed in next to Emmaline so that they could both be seen in the video chat window. They sat at Emmaline's desk in front of her open laptop.

"It's my pleasure," Dr. Alena Sokolová answered, clearly intrigued by the message that had been waiting for her when she woke up that morning.

Emmaline had begun her research the night before, trying to find an entomologist that they could talk to. It didn't take her long to discover, though, that she was on the wrong track. Ticks, she learned, were not insects, but arachnids. And as such they needed to make contact not just with an arachnologist, but better yet one that specialized in the subfield of acarology. She had also found contact info for researchers at Georgia Southern University, the Australian National Insect Collection, the Acarology lab at Ohio State University, and the Tick Research Lab at Texas A&M. But Dr. Sokolová at the Institute of Parasitology in the Czech Republic was the first to respond back to her.

Before the call, Emmaline reviewed some of Dr. Sokolová's online lectures. She had been particularly disgusted by one video featuring a close-up computer simulation of the feeding ritual of ticks.

"The tick feeds by securing itself onto the host with its sharp mouthparts," the Czech scientist's voice had said over the video of a tick settling onto a human arm. Its hard scutum—Emmaline had never heard that word before that night—shielded the upper portion of its body while feeding on the host.

"Note how the sensory palps both protect the mouthparts that are directly responsible for feeding, as well as help the tick find a suitable spot to imbed itself," she continued over images of a tick's twitching palps, two fat, finger-like appendages flanking its more fearsome feeding parts. When the palps parted, they revealed a second pair of oral appendages that resembled medieval weapons: long saber-like extensions covered with hooks and barbs and sharp, spear-like tips that proceeded to cut and rip into the skin.

"The tick's chelicerae dig and tear at the flesh," Dr. Sokolová continued, "until they have created a breach sufficiently large for introduction of the hypostome for feeding." Here, something akin to a tongue—though covered like a cactus with more hooks and barbs—extended out from between the chelicerae, inserted itself into the fissure in the skin, and anchored itself there.

"And then," the Czech scientist concluded lightly, "like a child sipping at a straw, the tick sucks its host's blood through its hypostome for nourishment and survival."

Emmaline had stopped the video there.

"As I mentioned in my email, we have some questions about ticks," Emmaline explained, "and we're hoping you can help us out."

"Of course," the forty-ish researcher answered through a pronounced Czech accent.

"We live in a heavily wooded area in the midwestern region of the United States," Jackson explained, "and I recently encountered a massive tick in the forest here. I may have killed it, but we're obviously concerned, as it's nothing like we have ever seen before."

Dr. Sokolová perked up as she listened to Jackson.

"That's quite worrying," she answered. "Giant ticks are not native to the United States," she noted. "It is extremely rare to find one there."

"So there really are giant ticks, then?" Jackson asked, relieved to learn he wasn't crazy.

"Yes, certainly," the scientist replied. "The *hyalomma marginatum* is commonly known as the 'giant' or 'camel' tick. They are widely found in northern Africa and Asia, but it's not uncommon in recent years to find them in several parts of both Eastern and Western Europe." She paused. "They are very dangerous."

Jackson glanced at Emmaline: *See!*

"Yes," he confirmed. "The one I found here has killed several large animals, including some farm animals. Is that consistent with what you know of these ticks?"

"Indeed," she confirmed. "They can be deadly, not just for smaller animals, but for large animals, as well. And certainly for humans."

"That's remarkable," Jackson said, though a part of him would have preferred to have been wrong. "I have to admit, even I was beginning to have my doubts, even though I saw it with my own eyes."

"Yes, but I had to be amused," she continued, her English getting just a bit awkward, "when you said that one killed several large animals. I highly doubt that one tick, even a *hyalomma marginatum,* could be responsible for more than one large mammal."

"What do you mean?"

"These ticks, like others, are parasites. Bloodsuckers. They track and attack a host and then drain blood to feed themselves. You mentioned livestock, which are particularly attractive to the *hyalomma marginatum* because they can support large infestations, oftentimes of one hundred or more."

"One hundred what?" Jackson asked.

"One hundred ticks," Dr. Sokolová answered.

"Wait, wait, wait," Jackson insisted. "You're saying that there may be one hundred of these things out there?"

"Well," the doctor continued, "I can't know for sure, of course, but if there has indeed been some migration to North America, I wouldn't be surprised."

Emmaline broke into the conversation. "And how would that migration occur?"

On the video screen, Dr. Sokolová shrugged.

"I'm not sure, really. Spread in our part of the world has occurred primarily when one of these ticks attaches to a migratory bird or something of that nature and is carried many hundreds of miles. To reach the United

States, I'd guess that—"

"Hold on," Jackson cut her off. "How would one of these things ride a *bird*?"

"I don't understand," Dr. Sokolová replied. "*Ride a bird*?"

"The one that attacked me was practically three feet across," Jackson shrugged. "How is that going to ride on the back of a bird?"

Dr. Sokolová laughed.

"I'm sorry," she said. "I pride myself on my good English, but I misunderstood what you just said. Perhaps I don't understand an American colloquialism, but the literal interpretation of what you just said would be a tick that measures nearly a full meter."

Emmaline and Jackson glanced at each other, both shrugging slightly.

"We're not really metric system people," Jackson answered, "but that sounds about right. A meter."

Dr. Sokolová was now thoroughly confused.

"I'm sorry, are you meaning centimeter or millimeter?"

"No," Jackson was starting to become agitated, "like you said initially. A *meter*."

"You're saying," the scientist said slowly, "that you saw a tick that was a meter long?"

"Yes, I told you it was massive."

"Massive, you said, not fantastical," she responded. "Yes, the *hyalomma marginatum is a 'giant tick'. It sometimes measures up to one-and-one-half centimeters in length. The largest ever confirmed was three centimeters, fully engorged with blood after feeding. That's the size of a walnut, not a...sofa seat. I'm sorry, but what you're describing is completely absurd. It's...I don't know another English word for it beyond absurd.*"

"Please, Doctor, you have to believe me. I saw this thing." He pointed to Emmaline. "It was as close to me as she is right now. How can we convince you?"

Something in his tone gave Dr. Sokolová pause.

"It's really quite ridiculous, but if you're sincere, get a picture of the creature and send it to me. If it does exist, it would be an extraordinary mutation."

"Well, I'm not enthusiastic about going out there and looking for it again," Jackson confessed. "It was extremely aggressive."

"Aggressive?"

"It attacked me unprovoked," Jackson explained. "Even after I shot it, it kept coming forward. I don't know how exactly to explain it, but once I fought back, I got the impression that it wasn't just after food. It was after me."

Dr. Sokolová didn't respond.

"What's wrong?" Jackson probed.

"Well, of course, the whole thing is entirely unbelievable," she responded, "but what you're describing is not behavior one would expect from a tick."

"How so?"

"Ticks are not aggressive in the way that we recognize that trait in other species," she explained, "like some insects or even some other arachnids. They lack the complex neural systems and behavioral patterns that manifest an attribute like aggression. In the same way, they don't organize in hierarchical structures like social insects do, for example. So, if this creature you claim to have encountered displayed signs of what we think of as aggression, then it suggests that its mutation goes beyond size. It suggests that it might act or behave or organize in ways that we would never expect from a common tick."

"But you don't believe it exists?" Emmaline pressed.

"No, of course I don't," Dr. Sokolová confirmed. "But as a scientist, what I believe or don't believe is completely evidence based. If you show me evidence, I will re-evaluate." She paused. "What about these animals you say it killed. Can you send me photos of any of its…victims?"

Emmaline and Jackson exchanged glances again but frowned.

"We haven't been able to get pictures to this point," Emmaline said, "but we can try. If it's still out there—" she looked over at Jackson, "—it's probably going to wander back to one of those farms for another meal."

Jackson nodded.

"Bear with us, Doc," he urged. "We'll reach out when we have more to go on, but please don't delete our emails. I promise you I'm not crazy."

"Well, it might make me the crazy one," Dr. Sokolová laughed, "but I'll keep my eyes open for those pictures. I promise you that if you send me something, I'll give it my immediate attention."

The three of them said their goodbyes.

"What do you think?" Jackson asked as soon as Emmaline disconnected the video call.

"Honestly, I think that's the best we're going to get."

"I think so too," Jackson agreed. "So we need to find some pictures."

"What do you have in mind?"

Chapter 14

CLAIRE MADSEN OPENED THE OVEN and, using a towel to protect her hand, pulled out the upper rack. Then she poked a wooden toothpick into a freshly baked brownie, slid it out, and examined it. A few wet crumbles clung to it, with just a bit of chocolate smearing, but no wet batter. This batch was done.

Using the towel to pick up the hot pan, Claire looked around the kitchen. Baked goods rested on several surfaces, and the entire house was filling with the sweet smell of chocolate. She wasn't sure where she was going to put these brownies down to cool.

Each year, Claire and six of her fellow farm wives ran a baked goods booth at the Jubilee. They called it the Tomahawk Hollow Helping Hands Bake Sale. Proceeds from their sales went to farm families that might be having a bad year or were facing unexpected expenses. Their yummy desserts, sweet breads, and other goodies were always popular with community members and tourists alike, and Claire was certain that this year would be their best yet.

It was a cool September day, and Claire had the window over the kitchen sink open to let some air in.

Oh well, she thought, *that's as good a place as any.*

Claire crossed the room and was about to set the pan on the windowsill when she stopped. Outside she could see Jake running through the soybean field toward the house as fast as his sixty-two-year-old legs could carry him. Waist-deep in the growth, he struggled to pass through, the stalks and leaves impeding his progress. Claire was startled by her husband's demeanor—Jake looked panicked as he ran—and absently tried to set the pan down, only to send it crashing into the sink.

Claire went to the back door and swung it open. Jake's alarm only grew when he spotted her, and he waved his hands wildly.

"Get back in the house!" he hollered, never breaking stride. Between running and shouting, though, the exertion began to overtake him and he slowed considerably.

"Jake!" Claire cried. "What's wrong?"

"Get back in the—" he started to repeat, but his terrified command was suddenly cut off. Arms flailing, Jake went pitching forward and disappeared into the thick expanse of pale green soybean leaves. Claire saw him fall even before his agonized scream reached her ears.

Her own chest now tight with dread, Claire stepped forward off the back step, ready to run to Jake's aid. But then she saw something that stopped her in her tracks. As Jake cried out and struggled out of sight in the field, a dark shape rose above the stalks, seemingly climbing right on top of him. There was a squall of frantic activity, and then Jake screamed again, this time in agony. In an instant, what had just been a wild, frenzied mele ended, and the dark form sank slowly into the crops.

A cry rose in Claire's throat, but even before she could release it, her terror stopped her again. Not far from where Jake fell, Claire could see something strange happening in the soybean field. Even as the area around Jake had grown still, two paths seemed to be cutting themselves through the field...along a line that would take them directly to where Claire was standing.

Claire knew instinctively that whatever had gotten Jake, there were more of them out there. And whatever they were—wild animal or something even worse—they were now burrowing through the field towards her. Claire retreated into the house and slammed the door behind her. With trembling fingers, she fumbled with the lock, determined to secure the house. Just as the lock clicked into place, something hammered into the door with such a powerful thump it sent her jolting backwards.

Turning to flee, Claire slammed into the kitchen table, sending herself—along with plates and pans of chocolate delights—crashing to the floor. As she scrambled to get to her feet, there was movement by the sink. What she saw overwhelmed her with terror. Something more horrific than anything she could ever imagine was trying to crawl through the open window. Claire just gaped at it in revulsion.

Two of the tick's long spindly legs reached into the kitchen, its claws flailing impotently as the creature jammed itself in the window frame. Apart from those front legs, only its head had yet fit through opening. Its fat, quivering palps opened and closed as it tried to see and sense its prey. As Claire backed away from it, those palps spread wide, and the frightful, jagged chelicerae extended towards her. Slime dripped from the sharp barbs on the fearsome oral appendages, but they weren't long enough to reach Claire, who stumbled backwards away from it.

The freakish beast shuddered and thrashed as it tried to force its way in, but its body was too big for the opening.

Claire turned and fled.

As soon as she entered the living room, she saw that her escape would be cut off. Through the large picture window over the sofa, she could see another of the relentless monsters mount a chair on the porch and prepare to ram itself against the window. It did, and the glass shattered inward, raining jagged shards over Claire, who screamed again.

Disoriented from the collision, the giant tick scuttled about on the floor. Another of its kind followed it through the demolished window.

Claire fled again, this time to the staircase. She mounted it and struggled up to the second floor on her frail, trembling legs. The two ticks pursued up the stairs clumsily but with astonishing conviction. Their front claws slashed at her feet as she went, first into the upstairs hallway and then into their master bedroom.

Breathless, Claire slammed the bedroom door, but the closest tick was already halfway in. The door banged into its head and swung wide open once more.

Again, Claire's survival instinct pointed her to the only exit, this time an open window over the bed. She crawled onto the mattress and forced open the window. Behind her, the two ticks scuffled over which would be the first through the door, but soon the clicking of their deadly appendages on the hardwood floor announced their pursuit.

Facing out toward the back soy field, Claire hesitated. There was only a small angling of roof for her to climb onto. From there it would be at least a fourteen-foot jump to the ground below. The thought of it practically paralyzed the old woman.

That hesitation cost her.

A searing pain flared in her back as one of the ticks lashed out with its razored front leg. The shock and pain propelled her forward, and she half-fell, half-leapt from the window. Holding her breath, Claire dropped silently and quickly. Landing awkwardly, all her weight fell on her extended left leg, and it snapped like a brittle twig. She collapsed crippled onto the grass.

All at once, the piercing pitch of her scream returned, and she knew for certain that her effort to escape was over. Her leg ruined, hope drained out of her. She rolled over onto her side just in time to see two more of the monstrous things clattering towards her across the grass.

Claire Madsen died before the mindless, bestial fight over her blood even began.

Chapter 15

THE PHONE RANG FOR A Fifth time before it was finally picked up. Chief Donovan had tried the number twice earlier that morning but hadn't gotten an answer. Shuffling through some papers on his desk, he was about to hang up again when he heard the voice on the other end.

"Henry Wilson's office. Can I help you?"

Donovan plucked up the receiver.

"Yes, I'm actually trying to reach Carly Winters."

"This is Carly Winters," she replied. "Who's this?"

"This is Chief Tim Donovan of Tomahawk Hollow, Wisconsin, and I'm trying to determine the whereabouts of Henry Wilson."

The other end of the line went silent for so long that Donovan wondered if they'd been disconnected.

"Ms. Winters?"

"Yes, I'm sorry." Carly cleared her throat. "Henry's missing?"

"It appears so, yes," Donovan answered, pausing a moment to see if she would volunteer anything. She didn't. "I understand you've been trying to reach him without success, is that correct?"

"Yes."

Again, Donovan waited for more, but nothing more was forthcoming.

"And when did you speak with him last?" Donovan asked.

"Two days ago. Tuesday afternoon."

"And what were the circumstances of that call?"

"Circumstances?"

"Ms. Winters," Donovan said calmly but firmly, "this doesn't need to be so hard. What were the circumstances of that call? Did you call him? Did he call you? What was it about? I have a wife and three kids here in town who are very worried, and any information you can provide would be very much appreciated."

Carly cleared her throat again, and when she spoke, her voice cracked slightly. "Yes, I'm sorry. We were texting about a, um, case that he's in the middle of. And I needed some information for the client. I think he was out for a run when I reached him."

"And who was this client?" Donovan probed.

"I can't tell you that," Carly answered.

"Of course. What is the case about?"

"I'm sorry, but I can't tell you that, either."

"I see." Donovan paused. "So, your last contact with him was a text message?"

Carly hesitated, about to answer, but stopped herself.

"Ms. Winters, please," Donovan pressed.

"I'm sorry," Carly exhaled deeply. "Yes, we were texting, and then I tried calling to, um, clarify something. But I didn't reach him."

"He didn't answer?"

"Well, he answered," she replied, "but I don't think he could hear me."

"Why not?"

"He just wasn't responding."

"I don't understand," Donovan said.

"He just seemed to be in some sort of..." She seemed unsure how to say it. "...distress."

"Distress? What kind of distress?"

"I, I really don't know," Carly stammered, sounding on the verge of tears, "I couldn't hear very well, but he, he seemed...in distress."

"Ms. Winters," Donovan began, "why are you just reporting this now? Why didn't you tell his wife when you spoke to her yesterday?"

Carly broke into a full sob on the other end of the line.

"Look, miss," Donovan said gently, "I don't give a damn about his private life, and I certainly don't give a damn about yours. I'm not investigating anyone's personal behavior. I'm just trying to find a missing person."

"I know, I'm so sorry," Carly sputtered, trying to compose herself. "He sounded so *scared*."

"Scared?"

"He was crying out, I don't know why," Carly said. "Something was terribly wrong…and then it seemed like he was just…gone."

Chief Donovan rubbed his temple and sighed. Things were getting worse in Tomahawk Hollow by the day.

#   #   #

Before Emmaline even got out of her car, she knew something was wrong.

From the driveway, she could see the overturned furniture on the porch and the smashed picture window leading into the living room. Her pulse was already racing as she advanced toward the house and saw that there was no shattered glass littering the porch. Clearly, the window had been broken from the outside.

The Madsen farm was her third stop this morning after starting at the Becker and Lupinski farms first. Neither of them had been eager to speak with her, but they both assured her there had been no further incidents after the ones they reported. She had no reason to disbelieve them. However, Emmaline also got the distinct feeling that she was being given the bum's rush. The normally friendly farmers seemed unusually curt and impatient with the young reporter.

Emmaline had hoped that she'd have better luck with Claire Madsen. Now, though, advancing the story was the least of her concerns. She just wanted to find Claire and Jake safe in their home.

Concerned for the Madsens but leery of entering the farmhouse without knowing what waited inside, Emmaline passed by the porch and moved around to the side of the house. As her reluctant feet carried her toward the backyard, she couldn't help but notice the Tomahawk Hollow Pesticides plant off in the distance. It hovered just beyond the boundary of the Madsens' fields. No matter where you went in Tomahawk Hollow, the shuttered factory always seemed to be right there, either literally or figuratively. But this morning especially, as Emmaline had made her rounds, she realized that the farms that had reported lost livestock that week were all in relatively close proximity to Tomahawk Hollow Pesticides.

Emmaline rounded the house into the backyard and froze. Her stomach knotted, bile rising in her throat. Even at that distance, there was no mistaking the broken, twisted human corpse lying in the grass behind the house. It was the remains of Claire Madsen, and Emmaline gagged once. It was all she could do to stop from emptying her stomach onto the ground at her feet.

Shaken, Emmaline covered her mouth with her hand. She had never seen a dead body outside of a funeral home before, and certainly never one that had been so savagely violated. Despite the revulsion that suddenly gripped her, Emmaline approached the bloody mess.

The closer she got, the more horrifying the scene became. Despite the red-stained grass, the state of the farm wife's remains was eerily similar to the slaughtered livestock at the Becker farm. Claire Madsen had been drained of her blood.

Emmaline's mind raced over the series of pictures she'd looked at while researching blood-sucking arachnids. Involuntarily, she pictured one of those ugly bugs—swollen to enormous proportions—mounting a screaming Claire Madsen, stabbing her in the chest, and drinking her blood.

Stop it, Emmaline, she scolded herself, *that's ridiculous.*

But what else could have done this?

Standing over the corpse, Emmaline fumbled with her Canon camera. She had always been a better writer than photographer, but modern news was reported in pictures and videos, not words. With one hand steadying the camera and the other focusing the lens, Emmaline snapped away liberally, taking shot after shot of the mutilated corpse.

There's no way Tim can stop us from making these public, she assured herself, stopping only after she had recorded dozens of digital photos.

When she finished with the pictures, she glanced around the back of the house, the field, and the barn, searching quickly for any evidence of what might have happened here. Her reporting instincts had begun to overcome her disgust. Despite knowing she still might be in danger herself, she wanted to make a thorough investigation of the property.

As her eyes scanned around, Emmaline noticed some disturbance to the crops at the edge of the soy field. She took two steps towards it, and then stopped. Glancing back at Claire's remains, Emmaline thought for a moment and then reached for her cell phone.

Chapter 16

THE LATE-MORNING AIR REMAINED crisp in Tomahawk Woods thanks to the natural forest canopy providing shade to so many of the trails. Even as the morning got later and the sun rose higher in the sky, the trails remained pleasant and mild. Had it not been for the disagreeable company, Dan Butler might have actually been enjoying the woods.

"Do you have any idea at all where you're going?" Dan complained, wondering—and not for the first time—if they were searching for a needle in a haystack.

Elmer Dobbs just trudged forward, opening his mouth only to launch another brown rope of spittle to the forest floor. Dan followed, growing more agitated by Elmer's silence.

"Elmer!" he repeated, raising his voice.

But Elmer lumbered on.

After another ten minutes, Elmer stopped unexpectedly, raising a hand to signal "halt" like he was the leader of a Marine unit marching through enemy territory.

"Wha—" Dan began, but Elmer slashed his hand sharply through the air: *Shut up!*

Dan felt his pulse quicken, wondering what unseen danger Elmer might be detecting. Elmer raised his index finger and slowly pointed it at a spot in the trees about thirty feet away. Following the line with his eyes, Dan tried to discern what Elmer was seeing. For a moment, he saw nothing, and then—startling him—the branches started to rustle.

Dan caught his breath in his chest and held it, determined now not to make any sound at all. His anxiety deepened when he saw Elmer's hand drop to his side, feel for his handgun, and deftly unfasten the strap securing it in its holster. Elmer's fingers curled around the grip, slipping the gun free and positioning his index finger against the trigger. With his other hand, he disengaged the safety and then leveled the weapon toward the movement in the trees.

Starting to feel his legs go wobbly, Dan could barely contain himself. His mind raced, *What the hell is in those trees?*

Between their inability to find David and Cheri, that slaughtered deer, and Elmer's erratic behavior, Dan began to fear the worst. Not just for the kids, but suddenly for himself and Elmer, as well. Now something was about to burst through the forest wall, and his normally unshakable companion was white as a sheet.

Elmer pulled back the gun's hammer.

Dan braced himself.

And then it appeared.

A porcupine.

A regular, ordinary porcupine, waddling out of the underbrush, followed by two pups.

Exhaling, Dan felt relief wash over him. He laughed nervously.

Elmer looked over, also letting the tension drain out of him. He aimed the gun at the ground, re-engaged the safety, and then slowly lowered the hammer back into place.

"Sorry about that," he mumbled, surprising them both with the apology.

Dan eyed Elmer closely. He was entirely unnerved by how shaken the burly outdoorsman was by their innocuous encounter with the woodland family. Long after the prickly rodents had waddled back into the underbrush, Elmer was still gathering himself. Dan had no idea what Elmer had expected to emerge from the woods, but it certainly wasn't a harmless family of porcupines.

"What the hell are you so afraid of?"

\#   \#   \#

Donovan nearly knocked over a long-haired grandmother as he waded through the crowd in the lobby of the Main Street Inn. The check-in line snaked back all the way to the front door, and the couches and chairs were chock-full of tourists waiting for their rooms. With a curt apology, Donovan moved through the crowd, eyes darting around.

"Ashley!" he called out, interrupting an animated conversation between the hotel manager and a father of four unhappy with his family's accommodations.

"Chief," she greeted with a tense smile.

Ashley Clark had started working at the Main Street Inn when she was sixteen years old. At first she was just a gopher after school and on the weekends, but when she graduated high school she also graduated to the front desk. An extrovert and a problem solver, she soon moved up the ranks, taking online courses to better understand the industry. And when tourism started to become Tomahawk Hollow's stock-in-trade, Ashley was promoted to hotel manager just a week shy of her twenty-eighth birthday.

"This is Mr. Miller," Ashley continued. "He and his family came all the way from the Twin Cities. Mr. Miller, this is Chief Donovan."

"Excuse me," Donovan said with a perfunctory nod. "I just need to borrow Ashley quick."

"Well, excuse *me*. We're in the middle of something here," the exasperated father protested. Donovan ignored him, taking Ashley by the arm and moving her three steps away.

"Is everything okay, Chief?"

"Sorry, Ash," Donovan apologized, "I know it's a crazy day."

"It's okay," she assured. Then, with a knowing smile, she lowered her voice to a conspiratorial whisper, "Is this about the creeper in room 217?"

"What?"

"You know," she giggled. "Lurch. In room 217. The guy who looks like he should be running errands for the Addams Family."

With all that was going on, Donovan had nearly forgotten about the bizarre stranger he'd seen at check-in the day before. Apparently, though,

Donovan hadn't been the only one who noticed his arrival in town.

"Oh right, that guy," Donovan said. "What's his story?"

Ashley giggled again, "Who knows? It's not like he's been chatting up the staff."

"I suppose not."

"I did see him talking to the mayor last night, though," Ashley noted, that conspiratorial tone returning. "And I don't think they were discussing the Miss Harvest Moon pageant."

"*Excuse me*," the Minnesota Millers grumbled, growing increasingly impatient.

Donovan raised a finger and snapped at Mr. Miller, "Just one minute!"

"The mayor," he continued, turning back to Ashley and his original business, "that's who I'm looking for. Have you seen him around t his afternoon?"

"Yeah," Ashley nodded. "He was in just a bit ago shaking hands. He's probably still around Main Street somewhere doing his thing."

"Alright," Donovan said, rubbing his head. "Thanks, Ash. If he comes back, tell him I need to see him, okay?"

"Will do, Chief," Ashley promised, and Donovan headed towards the door.

Taking a deep breath, Ashley ran her hands over her shirt to smooth away the wrinkles and then turned back to her problem guest. "Okay, Mr. Miller. Where were we?"

Chapter 17

BROWN SPITTLE DRIBBLED DOWN ELMER Dobbs' chin as he stared down his companion and gathered himself.

Dan was a pain in the ass, but Elmer was beginning to think that he deserved to know. Elmer leaned forward and pushed the chewing tobacco out of his mouth, spitting out the remainders before he spoke.

"I used to work up at the plant," Elmer began, letting the statement hang there portentously.

"So?" Dan shrugged.

"You know what they did up there?"

"At Tomahawk Hollow Pesticides? Yeah, I think they made *pesticides*."

"That's not all they did."

"Okay, fine, what else did they do?"

"I was on the plant floor, mostly," Elmer explained, "but now and then I made extra bucks helpin' out on special projects."

For the first time, Dan was intrigued. "What kind of special projects?"

Elmer took a deep breath, finally deciding just to give him the whole story.

"The place was owned by a foreign outfit, I don't know where from," Elmer began. "People 'round town didn't know, but lotta us could tell. Lotta foreigners in suits comin' through, you know? Not talkin' English.

"The pesticide stuff was legit. They sold it all 'round. Pretty good product, I guess. Least that's what the farmers 'round here said. Better than a lotta the shit out there these days. But it weren't their main thing. What they was really doin' was research."

Dan scowled. So far, this had been an awful lot of buildup for the revelation that this company was doing R & D.

"So what? There's nothing wrong with a company working on new products."

"Not pesticides," Elmer continued. "They were experimentin' with animals. Growth stuff. Hormones or somethin'."

"Like, BGH?" Dan speculated.

"I dunno," Elmer explained, "but it wasn't about getting' more milk outta cows. I'm talkin' *experiments*. Like, in the basement. Locked doors. Illegal stuff."

"If you know this, why did you—"

"Me and some of the other guys from the plant," Elmer continued, "we was just extra hands. Clean-up, mostly. *Disposal*, they called it."

"Disposal?" Dan didn't like the sound of that.

Elmer glared at him, reluctant to continue.

But he'd gone this far already.

"They were doin' stuff with mice, rats, that sorta thing, least what I could tell," Elmer continued. "I never seen what they were doing, really. But one time," he hesitated, knowing how it would sound, "they sent me to take a bag to the burn room. Someone said it was a rat." He paused. "I didn't open it, but just carryin' that thing, it was bigger than any rat I ever heard of. Like…five or six times bigger."

"Elmer, come on…"

"I'm tellin' you," Elmer snapped. "They made these things. Watch 'em grow. And then burn 'em up."

Dan shook his head. Elmer's story sounded crazy.

"Look, Elmer…" Dan was trying to reason with him. "If you didn't open the bag, how could you know for sure? You never actually saw it, right?"

Elmer hesitated, but Dan pressed him, "Right?"

"No," Elmer admitted, "I never looked in that bag."

"Okay, then," Dan continued, "then you don't—"

"But I sure as hell saw the one got loose."

Dan stopped. His mouth hung open.

"What?" Dan gasped.

"I still can't figure how it got out. One tech guy got killed right there in the lab. Another got her arm bit off. A couple of them foreigners. The thing got out somehow and disappeared into the woods."

"These woods?" Dan imagined a giant rat lurking just out of sight in the trees. "You think it's out here somewhere?"

Elmer ignored him.

"They grabbed up eight guys who grew up 'round here and told us to get it back. Jed Hammill and Erik Johnson found it and shot it up good. But that damn thing was still breathin' when we hauled it back to the plant. Big around as one of the tires on my truck. I saw it go into that incinerator with my own eyes, so I know it ain't out here no more."

Elmer paused. To calm his nerves—or maybe to reward himself for finally telling his story—he shoveled another pinch of chewing tobacco under his lower lip.

"Three days later they shut down the plant," Elmer concluded. "Me and the other special projects guys got ten grand for our trouble. I never saw none o' them foreign fellas again."

Dan stared at Elmer. The story was incredible.

"You mean for your silence," Dan finally said.

"Huh?"

"You got ten thousand dollars for your silence, right? Not your *trouble*. I bet you signed papers and everything."

"So what if I did?"

The two men stood in silence for several long moments, both resenting the hell out of each other. Both wishing that circumstances had never stuck the two of them together.

"But if you found the rat," Dan finally asked, "why are you in such a panic out here?"

Elmer just glared at Dan.

"'Cause when you know what I know, you wonder what you *don't* know."

Chapter 18

"IT'S ME," EMMALINE SPOKE INTO her phone, making sure that she could be heard over the roar of her car engine.

"I found…I don't know," she sputtered. "God, my hands are shaking. I can barely drive. Drop whatever you're doing and meet me at the office!"

Hanging up, Emmaline dropped her phone onto the car seat and cranked the steering wheel around to turn up the long driveway. It hadn't taken her long after wading into the soy field to find Jake Madsen's remains. They were in the same state as Claire's, and after snapping off a dozen photos, Emmaline got the hell out of there.

Her intention had been to head right back to the Gazette. But as she pulled out of the Madsens' driveway, she caught sight of the shuttered pesticides plant in the distance once again. Having seen it repeatedly that morning as she made her rounds, her instincts told her it was more than just a coincidence. She was determined to check it out.

Now, though, as she wound up the driveway towards the plant, those same instincts started screaming at her to turn the car around. Up ahead, coming more clearly into view, Emmaline could see a black van parked near the abandoned plant's locked chain-link gate. Even more alarming: two men in dark suits stood guard in front of the gate.

Emmaline slowed the car but continued forward, pulling up right in front of the men. Neither made a move, and Emmaline watched them for a moment through the front windshield before sliding out of the car. Before she could approach the two motionless sentinels, she saw the side door of the van slide open and a third man climb out.

Even more so than the other two, there was something disconcerting about this tall, lanky stranger who strode up to Emmaline. She couldn't stop herself from taking a half step backwards, but he was on her quickly and hovering over her.

"Can we help you with something, miss?" Karl Kellerman asked in his strange voice, his eyes—as always—hidden behind those dark sunglasses.

Startled both by his physical appearance and the strange faux-American accent he was clearly putting on, Emmaline answered haltingly.

"I'm…I'm a reporter with the Tomahawk Gazette," she asserted, perhaps thinking that the statement would carry more weight than it did. She cleared her throat. "I'm here to follow up on a story."

Kellerman studied Emmaline silently through his shades. After a moment, his lips curled into a tight smile. "You're an Indian," he stated, oddly pleased.

Normally, Emmaline would have corrected his outdated terminology, but the strange declaration caught her so off guard that she simply shrugged. "So?"

His thin smile widened just a bit. "I have never encountered a real American Indian before. Your features are very distinctive."

Baffled by the strange interaction, Emmaline tried to regain her footing. "What are you guys doing out here?"

"We are a private security firm employed by the property owners."

"It's an abandoned plant that's been empty for years—"

"I'm afraid I cannot allow you inside," Kellerman interrupted.

Emmaline tried to see through this stranger's dark glasses to his eyes, but they were entirely opaque. She glanced over at the other two men, neither of whom appeared to have moved an inch since she'd arrived. For the first time she realized that both men had weapons slung behind their backs. She couldn't see the guns themselves, but the straps crossed their chests, with cartridges of ammunition clipped to them. Emmaline quickly abandoned any fantasy of trying to get past them.

"I thought that Tomahawk Hollow Pesticides went out of business," she said, turning her attention back to Kellerman. "Who are the property owners?"

This time, Kellerman ignored her question entirely, simply repeating, "I'm afraid I cannot allow you inside."

Realizing that she wasn't going to get any answers from this man, Emmaline decided on a tactical retreat. Without another word, she opened the door, climbed in, and began to close the door. Kellerman's hand caught it and held it open.

"Access to the property will be prohibited indefinitely," he stated, now leaning over her. "Do not return."

Emmaline took it exactly how he meant it.

As a warning.

Without answering, she tugged at the door. Kellerman let it go, and the door banged shut. Emmaline pulled away just as quickly as she could.

As the car pulled back down the driveway, Emmaline saw the man watch her go through her rearview mirror. Just before she turned the bend out of sight, she saw him reach into his jacket pocket and pull out his cell phone.

#   #   #

Mayor Cankerby walked up Main Street reviewing the work of the city's staff and volunteers. With the start of the festival just one day away, preparations were in their final stages. Taking pride in how the community worked together to make these events a success, the mayor was using the opportunity to hand out a generous helping of compliments and congratulations. At the same time, he was glad-handing the tourists and pointing them in the direction of various local businesses to patronize and support during their visit to Tomahawk Hollow.

But the call on his cell phone put a quick end to his good cheer.

The caller's number was blocked, and the mayor knew what that meant.

He frowned, answering the phone. "Yes? What is it?"

It was Kellerman's voice on the other end of the line. "An Indian girl was just trying to get into the site. She said she is a reporter."

"Christ, Emmaline," Cankerby breathed. "What the hell was she doing out there?"

"We turned her away," Kellerman reported.

"For that matter, what the hell are *you* doing out there?"

"I have my orders," Kellerman responded without emotion. "What do you want me to do about the girl?"

Mayor Cankerby huffed. At this point, it wasn't going to be enough to hold off Jackson and Emmaline until after the festival. He could see that a more permanent solution was going to be necessary.

"I think it's time," the mayor sighed, "to neutralize the Gazette, per our earlier discussion."

"I'll take care of it," Kellerman confirmed.

"I need you to understand—" the mayor began, but he was quickly cut off.

"SILAS!'

Mayor Cankerby stopped and looked around. Not far away, Chief Donovan jogged towards him waving a hand.

"I have to go," Cankerby said into the phone. "Just get it done."

The mayor hung up and pocketed his phone just as Donovan caught up with him.

"Hello there, Tim," greeted the mayor, endeavoring to maintain his broad smile despite the chief's clear agitation.

"We may have a bigger problem than we thought," Donovan chuffed, catching his breath after running down Main Street.

The mayor glanced around, trying to determine if any passersby were within earshot.

"I've got a missing tourist now, too," Donovan continued, "and I'm worried it might be—"

The mayor's broad smile flickered away.

"Keep your voice down, dammit!" he snapped. "What the hell are you talking about?"

Donovan glanced around himself.

"A lawyer from Chicago," he explained, his voice lower now. "His wife and kids left him at their rental the other afternoon, and when they came back he was gone. His girlfriend thinks she heard something happen to him when he was out for a run."

"Girlfriend? You just said wife!"

Donovan sighed. "He's here with his wife and family. His girlfriend is back in Chicago."

"Oh for God's sake." The mayor's laugh was entirely devoid of humor. "Some big city hotshot abandons his family and is probably off diddling his *side piece*—" he grinned broadly, proud of his mastery of the current slang, "—and you fly off in a panic over it? Get it together, Chief."

"He's not with his girlfriend," Donovan clarified through gritted teeth, "and his family had to hire a car to take them back to Chi—"

"Look," the mayor wouldn't let him finish. "You're the goddamned Chief of Police, so if there's someone who needs to be arrested over this, you go ahead and arrest them! But don't come running hysterically down Main Street on a day like today squawking some cock-and-bull nonsense about how *this* is related to *that*!"

The chief simmered, biting his tongue to avoid further escalation of the suddenly tense confrontation.

"Now," the mayor continued, "if you have any confusion about what your job is here, go ahead and take some time to work through it. But do it while you're packing up your office. Because I will not hesitate to send you back to downtown Milwaukee or Racine or wherever the hell it was you were walking some *inner city beat* until I brought your underqualified, affirmative action butt up here to paradise. Do you understand, Chief?"

Donovan glared at the mayor.

"Yes, I understand, Silas," he growled. "Like I said, you're not subtle."

"Good. And for the last goddamn time, it's *Mr. Mayor*."

Chapter 19

EMMALINE'S HANDS STILL SHOOK AS she pulled her car to a stop a half block off Main Street. With the town's main artery already blocked off for the weekend's festivities, she'd have to walk a bit further than normal to get to the Gazette. But with her mind reeling from all the questions the past hour had triggered, her legs took her right past the front door of the Gazette and put her on a path toward City Hall. She wouldn't be able to find all the answers there, but she would get a good start.

"I need to see a deed, Miriam," Emmaline said to the staffer working the City Clerk's desk. In a town the size of Tomahawk Hollow, there was a lot of overlap in municipal functions, and in this case the City Clerk and the Registrar of Deeds were one in the same. Longtime city worker Miriam Todd was the person to talk to.

"What are you looking for, Em?"

"I'm trying to find out who owns the building and land out by the old pesticide plant."

"Hmmm. What do you need to know that for?" Miriam asked absently. Then, realizing, "Is this about the chemicals I told you about?"

"Just some background."

Miriam shrugged, got up from her desk, and walked back to the records room.

"I'll just be a minute," she said over her shoulder as she disappeared through the door.

Emmaline glanced around.

City Hall was practically empty, with most municipal staff already dispatched to make final preparations for the Jubilee. Other than Miriam, Emmaline spotted only one other city worker walking around. The door to the mayor's office was half-open, but she didn't see him or anyone else inside.

A minute later Miriam reappeared, walking back over to Emmaline with a scowl on her face.

"Well, that's strange," Miriam told her, retaking her post behind the desk.

"What?"

"That document's missing," Miriam said. "It's possible it was misfiled."

"That's pretty strange, don't you think?"

Miriam smiled. "Not really. Sometimes some of the—" she pointed her thumb upwards, "—*higher-up's* pull a file and then try to put it back themselves. And you can imagine how well that goes." She laughed. "There's a stack of documents to be re-filed," she continued, "but we're so short-handed today I can't really spend the time back there looking for it. Come back Monday?"

Emmaline chewed her lower lip.

"Would you mind taking a quick look through that pile, Miriam?" she asked. "It's really important. I wouldn't ask otherwise. I promise I'll stay right here and watch the door. If anyone comes in, I'll give a shout."

Shrugging, Miriam acquiesced. "Sure, Em, but if the mayor comes back, you get me right away. He's in a mood today."

Miriam returned to the records room, and Emmaline gave another quick glance around.

Higher-ups, Miriam had said. In Tomahawk Hollow, that usually meant one thing. With Miram occupied and Emmaline suddenly alone, she made a bee line for the mayor's office.

Peeking inside, Emmaline confirmed that the office was empty and then slipped inside. She closed the door just enough to block the view of any casual passerby, and then she went directly to the mayor's desk.

Several stacks of papers were on top of the desk. Emmaline quickly thumbed through them. Memos to review. Letters to sign. A timeline and rundown of the Harvest Moon Jubilee. But nothing about the pesticides plant.

Just as she finished examining the material on the desk, her phone rattled and beeped. She pulled it out quickly, immediately setting it to mute, and then looked at her text messages. Jackson was just a few minutes away from arriving at the office.

Placing her phone on the desk, she began tugging at its drawers. None were locked, but none held anything of note. Just piles of office supplies, a couple empty notebooks, official stampers, and the like. Emmaline moved things around trying to find anything that might offer some insight into anything, but no luck.

Disappointed, Emmaline looked around the office to see where she might search next. In the corner sat an old wooden filing cabinet. It was the kind of thing she would never have taken notice of in any other circumstance, but these weren't normal circumstances.

Moving around the desk, Emmaline went to the cabinet, passing by the open door. Just as she did, a city staffer walked past. Emmaline lurched behind the door to avoid being seen.

Emaline held her breath silently and watched through the crack between the door and the wall, but the staffer just kept on walking. A moment later, the main reception area was empty again, and Emmaline went to the filing cabinet.

Crouching in front of the squat two-drawer cabinet, Emmaline tugged at the top drawer. It didn't budge. Locked. Moving to the lower drawer, Emmaline gave it a pull, and to her delight it slid right open. Her excitement faded quickly, though, when she saw that the drawer was empty but for a single sheet of blank white paper lying at the bottom of the cabinet.

Emmaline cursed under her breath and shoved the drawer shut. As she did, she heard a faint scraping sound: something hard sliding across the floor of the drawer. Pulling it open again, she moved the white paper away, and underneath it was a key.

Her heart beating a bit quicker now, Emmaline picked up the key.

The mayor's not really that stupid, is he?

Emmaline thought he just might be.

She positioned the key at the lock of the top drawer, inserted it, and half-laughed as the key turned and the lock opened.

He is!

Inside, a fat, unlabeled file folder hung in the cabinet, and Emmaline reached for it eagerly. Just as she grabbed it, she heard the *ding-dong* of the lobby door opening. She glanced up. If Miriam heard it, too, she would likely come out to attend to the customer. Emmaline realized she only had a few seconds left before she'd have to get out of the office.

Opening the folder, she knew right away she wouldn't have time to examine all the contents. There was too much there to digest. Instead, she paged through quickly, searching for anything with the words "Tomahawk Hollow Pesticides" on it. She was unable to find anything so marked, but several different pages featured the name "Blutmond Holdings." In fact, it was on every page she saw. She knew she couldn't take the whole file—if the mayor checked the cabinet, he'd see it was gone—but Emmaline figured she could swipe one page with the name on it and it would never be missed. She plucked out a single page, dropped the file back into the drawer, and closed and locked it. Her heart now pounding out of her chest, she dropped the key into the lower drawer and closed that too.

Ready to make her escape, Emmaline stood up and turned towards the door, gasping out loud.

Mayor Cankerby was standing in the office doorway.

A furious scowl on his face, he spotted the contraband in her hand and snatched it away from her.

"What the hell are you doing?" he snapped.

Chapter 20

WHEN JACKSON ARRIVED AT THE Gazette and found the front door unlocked, he assumed that Emmaline had beaten him back to the office.

"Em!" he called out. Glancing around, he got no answer.

Jackson called out one more time, walking into his office as he checked his phone. No texts. He was still looking at his phone when he heard the voice.

"Mr. Reed."

Startled, Jackson dropped the phone but never saw it hit the floor. His eyes riveted to the pasty-skinned stranger in the black suit and sunglasses sitting behind his desk.

The strange man cracked a wan smile at seeing the jolt he had caused Jackson.

"Who the hell are you?" Jackson asked with as much authority as he could muster. In truth, he found the lanky stranger's appearance and affect distinctly unsetting.

"My name would be meaningless to you, Mr. Reed," Kellerman noted with a slow formality. "However, I represent certain concerns that I believe would interest you very significantly."

Curious but unwilling to let this intruder dictate their conversation, Jackson crouched to pick his phone up off the ground.

"I'm calling the police."

"Mr. Reed, please," Kellerman practically hissed, his smile widening. "That course of action will not be fruitful. Kindly listen to what I have to say, which you will soon find could be extremely beneficial to you. Chief Donovan has his hands full with the festival right now."

Surprised that the stranger knew the chief's name, Jackson hesitated. And as disconcerting as this stranger's bearing was to him, his curiosity had certainly been piqued.

"What do you want?" he tried again to seize control of the conversation.

"I understand, Mr. Reed," Kellerman began, "that your newspaper is significantly delinquent in its municipal tax payments and struggling to avoid financial insolvency."

Dammit, Silas, Jackson thought, *I should have known you were involved in this!*

"Look—"

"And I also understand, Mr. Reed," Kellerman cut in, "that—between your limited income, a contentious divorce some years back, and a fondness for nearby Indian gaming establishments—you personally are experiencing extreme financial distress. Which, given the feeble prospects of a failing business in a dying industry, you have little hope of ever reversing at this point in your life."

"Mister," Jackson began, "I'm not going to stand here—"

"And I further understand, Mr. Reed," Kellerman's voice rose this time, "that you, sir, have had a direct, personal encounter with a rather remarkable—" he articulated the next word for effect, "—*anomaly* in the forest."

That got Jackson's attention.

"What the hell do you know about that?" Jackson demanded.

Kellerman maintained his tight-lipped grin, though the dark glasses made his face entirely inscrutable.

"I know what it is, Mr. Reed."

Skeptical, Jackson challenged him, "Okay, so what is it?"

"A tick, Mr. Reed," Kellerman declared, enjoying being a step ahead of Jackson. "A giant tick."

The assertion caught Jackson off guard.

The only way this stranger could know that was if Cankerby or Donovan had told him, and Jackson was sure that neither of them had believed his story. So why would they have repeated it?

"Bullshit," Jackson snapped.

"Bullshit?" Kellerman repeated. "That is a curious response from a man who has claimed that it is just that."

"I don't believe that you know a damn thing about it."

"I know everything about it, Mr. Reed," Kellerman snapped. "I know what it is. I know where it came from. And I know how to find and kill it. Which is exactly what I was sent here to do."

Jackson hadn't noticed a large manila envelope sitting on this desk that didn't belong to him. But it drew his eyes now as Kellerman dug his fingers into it and pulled something out, throwing it onto the desk.

"And furthermore, Mr. Reed, I have a proposition," Kellerman continued calmly, "that I'm confident you will find very appealing."

Jackson exhaled sharply when he saw what it was.

Chapter 21

"TOMORROW MORNING. SEVEN O'CLOCK."

For the second time in two nights, Elmer Dobbs pulled his Ford truck into the driveway of Dan and Olive Butler's modest home at the end of a long, fruitless day. Both men were exhausted and frustrated. And their concern for their children, coupled with the prospect of spending a third day together tomorrow, had them both in a foul mood. Dan, in particular—who didn't care much for the outdoors to begin with and had a business to run—was just about at his wits' end.

"Elmer," Dan began, "I think we need to call Chief Donovan."

Elmer hadn't made eye contact with Dan since he finished his story that afternoon. Now he looked over sharply.

"Chief ain't gonna do nothin'," Elmer snapped. "He's got that wing ding this weekend to worry about. Besides, he's gonna say it's just kids bein' kids."

"I know," Dan continued, treading carefully, "but if you tell him your story—"

"Go to hell."

"Elmer, listen," Dan pressed. "If you tell him your story—tell him what you *saw*—he'll have to do something. What if one of those rats is still out there?"

"If I tell him that story, he's gonna lock me up," Elmer protested. "You said it yourself: I *signed*. I *signed* something saying I'd never talk about it. And if he don't lock me up for that, he's gonna lock me up for being crazy!"

"You can't be locked up for breaking an NDA," Dan laughed. "Don't be such a coward."

In an instant Elmer's fist found a handful of Dan's collar and pulled the smaller man halfway across the seat. Pressing his face up to Dan's, Elmer's rank, tobacco-fouled breath practically made the other's eyes water.

"You ever call me a coward again," Elmer growled, "I'll rip off that pint-sized pecker you got an' stuff it so far down your throat it'll come out one big chunk next time you take a crap! Hear me?"

"Okay! Okay! I'm sorry!" Dan exclaimed. Elmer immediately released him. "Jeez."

Elmer was no longer looking at Dan, but rather stared straight ahead through the front windshield.

"Seven tomorrow," Elmer repeated. "We're not comin' out of them woods again without our kids."

Dan climbed out of the truck, slammed the door behind him, and watched Elmer pull out onto the street.

With a deep sigh, Dan turned and saw Olive standing in the front doorway. She held a string of fat beads in her hands, fidgeting nervously.

"No luck again?" Olive asked as Dan climbed the front steps.

Dan put his hands on her shoulders and gave her a kiss on the cheek. He could see in her eyes that she was beginning to worry, as well.

"No."

Olive gave him a thin smile and nodded, beginning to turn back into the house.

"Well, alright then. Come in and have some supper."

Dan stopped her and gently turned her around to face him again.

"Olive," he began, his voice low, "we're going back out again tomorrow. After I leave, I want you to get in the car and go visit your sister in La Crosse. Go for a couple of days."

"Why?" she laughed, baffled by the odd request. "It's the Jubilee this weekend, for goodness sake!"

"Just listen to me, Olive," Dan insisted. "Go stay with Annie, and I'll call you when you can come home."

The bemused smile on Olive's face faded as she registered her husband's grave demeanor.

"Daniel Butler," she breathed. "What on earth is going on?"

Chapter 22

THE HARSH CLANK OF THE steel door slamming shut startled Emmaline awake. She jolted up just partially, but the ache from sleeping two hours on the metal bench stopped her.

"Em."

It was Donovan, finally.

Emmaline forced herself up this time. As annoyed as she was, she felt relief flood over her now that he had arrived to set her free.

When Mayor Cankerby had returned to his office late that afternoon, he had caught Emmaline red-handed, no two ways about it. She had been rifling through his files, and he was furious.

At first, Emmaline had stammered out an excuse, but he wasn't buying it. Next, she tried confronting him about her discoveries, but the more she tried to take the offensive, the more upset he got. Finally, she moved on to outrage as the mayor dragged her over to the police station. But when they got there and he deposited her into the holding cell, she realized that she would have to wait for Donovan to get back for any relief. That was six hours ago.

"What time is it?" Emmaline asked, still trying to shake the sluggishness from her awkward sleep.

"What in the hell were you thinking?" Donovan's sharp, angry tone caught her off guard, but it served to clear the last of the cobwebs.

Emmaline got up and walked across the one hundred square foot cell to where Donovan was standing just on the other side of the metal bars.

"Let me out of here," Emmaline said.

Donovan just stood there, arms crossed.

"I said let me out of here, Tim!" she insisted again, grabbing the bars with both hands as if to emphasize her imprisonment. Donovan was unmoved.

"You broke into the mayor's office, Em."

"Broke in? I didn't break in—"

"You were trespassing," he snapped, "and you stole official city documents. And on top of that, you explicitly disobeyed my—"

"*Disobeyed?*" It was Emmaline's turn to interrupt, this time incredulously.

"—direct order to stay the hell out of—"

"I don't have *obey* a damn thing you say, *Chief*!"

"—this!"

Donovan and Emmaline stood there glaring at each other through the bars.

"Come on Tim," Emmaline demanded for the third time. She tugged at the bars, as if she could cast them aside. "Let me out of here."

"You're not going anywhere, Em," Donovan replied, still angry but calmer now. "You're going to cool your jets in here until tomorrow, at least."

"What? You can't do that!" Emmaline objected. "I'm a reporter!"

Donovan just shrugged. "Then this should make a hell of a story. Tomorrow."

He turned and headed for the door, but Emmaline called out again, "Is this really how you're going to get back at me?"

That stopped him.

Donovan turned back around but didn't say anything. He just stared at her.

"I'm sorry, okay?" she blurted, but it didn't sound like much of an apology. "How many times do you want me to say it. I screwed up. But this is ridiculous! You can't let what happened between us—"

"Em, stop."

"He was my ex-fiancée!" she explained angrily, possibly for the tenth time. "You and I were fighting. I went home for my *nooka's* funeral…and you didn't come!"

"I have responsibilities here, Em. I can't just get up and leave without—"

"It was *mistake*, I know. I was confused. But it didn't have anything to do with you."

"It had a little to do with me, Em," Donovan answered wryly. He turned back again towards the door. "But nothing to do with this."

"Wait, Tim!" Emmaline tried to stop him again. "I was out at the Madsen farm—"

Again, he didn't let her finish.

"The mayor told me about your nutty claims about the Madsens," he interrupted, turning sharply back around, "and I already went out there. With everything going on around here, I have to waste my time on that bullshit, too?"

"What do you mean waste your time?"

"*Waste of time,*" he repeated. "There were no dead bodies. No broken windows. No sign of anything out of the ordinary. They're fine."

"You saw them?" Emmaline couldn't believe what he was saying.

"No," Donovan continued, "but Silas talked to them after he dumped you off in here. They had no idea what you were talking about."

"He's lying, Tim," Emmaline insisted. "They're not fine. They're both dead."

"Emmaline—"

"I have pictures!" she protested, raising her voice.

"Where?"

"On my camera, but Cankerby took it."

"Uh huh."

"And on my phone!"

"Okay," Donovan challenged. "So let's see them."

Emmaline's hand reflexively felt at her pocket, even though she already knew that the phone wasn't there. She'd discovered that earlier after the mayor had left her alone in the holding cell.

"I don't have it," she admitted. "I lost the phone. Or maybe the mayor took that, too. I can't remember."

"Well, there you go."

"Tim…"

But Donovan had already turned back towards the door.

"Good night, Em," he said coolly. "I'll be back in the morning."

"Tim!"

"Good night, Em."

And then he was through the heavy outer door and letting it clank shut behind him.

"TIM!" Emmaline bellowed one last time.

#   #   #

When Jackson opened his eyes, everything that had happened in the last few days was briefly forgotten. He was lying on the couch in his Gazette office, which was not unusual. With nobody to go home to since Winnie had left, he would often just crash at the office, particularly the night or two before a new edition was set to go to press. He glanced around in the dark, trying to recall what had kept him there overnight this time. Once he was able to break out of the deep sleep he had been in, it all came flooding back.

Pulling himself up into a sitting position, Jackson rubbed his head with both hands. He drew in a deep breath. Part of him—most of him—wished that he could forget again, but that was not going to be possible.

Jackson stood and crossed over to his desk, stepping carefully in the dark. He flicked on his desk lamp and dropped into his chair, pulling himself forward and resting his elbows on the surface. Once again, his hands massaged his aching temple.

In truth, his decision had already been made. In fact, it wasn't nearly as much of a dilemma as he thought it would be. As much as he thought it *should* be. It wasn't a question of right or wrong…or even idealism vs. pragmatism. It was simply a matter of there being only one path that he could take, and he was about to set off on it. Regardless, the whole thing had him tied up in knots. Was it self-doubt or a sudden bout of self-loathing? He wasn't sure. But he knew how to get rid of it.

Sliding open the file drawer next to him, Jackson reached in and pulled out a single clear glass and a nearly empty bottle of Jack Daniels. He screwed off the top, poured a couple fingers of the amber whiskey into the glass, and downed it in a single gulp. He poured two more fingers and set the bottle aside.

Next, Jackson opened the desk's middle drawer and removed a short stack of papers. He placed them on the desk in front of him. On top was a blank manila envelope, which he set aside. Then he paged through the other papers underneath. The electric bill. The phone bill. The property tax bill. The loan bill. Internet. Computer rentals. The accountant. And on and on. Half of them were boldly stamped "Past Due." Most of the others were more discreet but still late. Without enough money to even pay the bills, he personally hadn't been able to take a paycheck in months.

Reaching for the glass, Jackson swallowed it down in one gulp again and then refilled it with the last of the bottle. He raised it to his lips and then paused, exhaling deeply and setting the glass aside.

Instead, he reached for the envelope that the strange albino had left behind.

Jackson turned it over in his hands, considering it for a moment, and then his fingers pulled out the contents. He stared at it a long moment, re-reading the numbers as if to confirm to himself that it was what he thought it was.

As he stared at it, an electronic melody broke the silence.

Jackson looked up through his office door. He could see the dim light of Emmaline's laptop screen as it woke itself up to receive the video call.

Dropping the papers and picking up the whiskey glass, Jackson rose. He crossed his office to the door and exited to the outer office to see who was calling. It had to be past midnight, he figured. Who would be reaching out to Emmaline at such an hour?

When he reached her desk, Jackson was surprised to see the name of Dr. Alena Sokolová, the Czech acarologist, flashing on the computer screen. Intrigued, he sat down in front of the laptop and moved the cursor over the button to answer.

But he stopped himself before clicking.

Hold on a minute, he thought. *Just hold on.*

The musical alert continued insistently as Jackson sat there.

Finally, he raised the glass to his lips, swallowed the last of the Jack, and set the empty glass back down. Then he reached for the laptop and unceremoniously slammed it shut, casting the outer office back into silence and darkness.

Chapter 23

EVEN THE FAINT LIGHT OF dawn stung Emmaline's eyes as she exited the police station out onto Main Street. After spending the night in the dim, artificial glow and discomfort of Donovan's holding cell, she was sore, exhausted, and irritable. But now that Donovan had shown up again, opened the cell, and directed her out to the street, she was more confused than anything else.

The intrigue only deepened when she found Jackson, the mayor, and that mysterious albino waiting for her. Drab combat fatigues had replaced the stranger's black suit, but those dark glasses still covered his eyes.

"What the hell's all this?" Emmaline demanded, noting that two other pseudo-soldiers stood motionless near their van.

The mayor, his thousand-watt crocodile smile beaming, answered cheerily, "You're getting your wish, young lady. You get to publish your *blockbuster* story." He emphasized the word derisively. "That's what you wanted, wasn't it?"

Even though the Harvest Moon Jubilee would be kicking off later that day, Main Street was empty but for the odd collection of characters gathered around the black van. Soon the downtown would be teeming with volunteers, shopkeepers, and tourists, but now an eerie stillness and strangeness hung all around.

Not interested in the mayor's goading, Emmaline addressed her boss, "What's going on, Jackson?"

"I was right, Em," Jackson explained, his voice sounding odd and strained to Emmaline. "There's a giant tick in the woods that's been coming to the edge of town and killing livestock. These men are with a private security firm, and they're going to kill it."

"*Private security*," she repeated incredulously. "What's that a euphemism for?"

"Miss Blackdeer," the tall stranger's faux-American accent interrupted them. "My name is Karl Kellerman, and I assure that we are exactly who Mr. Reed says we are." He extended his hand for Emmaline to shake, but she wasn't interested. Kellerman lowered it.

"There is a...*creature*...in the forest," he went on, "which by now you are well aware of. It is our intention to track down this creature, destroy it, and ensure that your town is spared from any further...*inconvenience*."

"*Inconvenience*?" Emmaline spat. "People are dead because of that thing!"

"What?" Jackson was surprised. "What are you talking about?" The question was directed to Emmaline, but he was looking back and forth from Kellerman to the mayor for a response.

"The Madsens," Emmaline answered. "I saw them with my own eyes."

"Is this true?" This time Jackson was talking directly to Mayor Cankerby.

"Of course not!" the mayor scoffed. "Tim has been out to the farm twice now, and I personally spoke with Jake Madsen last night!"

"He's lying," Emmaline insisted, repeating the assertion she made to Donovan the night before. "He's just lying."

Jackson didn't know what to believe.

"None of this is interesting or relevant," Kellerman interjected. "We have a very pressing task at hand, and the sooner we can get to it, the less likely it will be that Miss Blackdeer's fevered dreams become a reality."

Emmaline glared at the tall man while Jackson tried to gather his thoughts. Kellerman, though, did not wait for either of them to respond, instead taking full charge of the situation.

"Now, Miss Blackdeer, you have a choice," Kellerman continued. "You can join us and your colleague here to observe and document our mission;

and when it is complete, you will be free to write and publish and report anything you wish about what you see. Or you can remain locked in that same cell until our task is complete and leave the journalistic work—and any potential notoriety sure to result from such a sensational story—to Mr. Reed alone. What you will not do, however, is interfere with or jeopardize our mission in any way."

Kellerman finished, letting his final words linger in the hazy space between declaration and threat.

Emmaline looked hard at Jackson, trying to understand what her mentor was thinking.

"You trust these guys?" she challenged, noting with a glance that the question triggered a thin smile from Kellerman.

"I think this thing needs to be killed," he replied carefully, "and I think that people need to know about it."

Emmaline scowled, realizing that Jackson's unresponsive answer was the best that she was going to get out of him.

"Fine."

"Excellent," Kellerman grinned joylessly. "Then let us not delay any further."

On cue, one of the two men standing by the van pulled open its sliding side door, waving a hand to usher Jackson and Emmaline inside. The other man climbed silently into the driver's seat.

Emmaline shot Jackson one more look: *Are you sure?*

Jackson nodded slightly and waited for Emmaline to pull herself into the van. Then he followed, slamming the door closed behind him.

As soon as it closed, Mayor Cankerby turned to Kellerman with a scowl.

"I trust you have this under control?" he asked softly, even though Emmaline and Jackson were well out of earshot.

Kellerman just stared back at him through his opaque sunglasses.

"You know, Kellerman," the mayor continued, "after you've cleaned up the mess in the woods, there's one more problem to deal with." The mayor let his eyes flicker over to look at the police station before returning quickly to Kellerman. "You understand?"

Even with his eyes hidden, it was difficult for Kellerman to mask his disdain for the insignificant local official. He took a half step towards the mayor and leaned in closely.

"Do not imagine for a moment, Mr. Mayor," Kellerman hissed, for the first time letting his voice betray a thick German accent, "that you have a better understanding of my vocation than I do. Do *you* understand *me*?"

Momentarily shaken, the mayor retreated back a step. He didn't answer, but he deflated just slightly, indicating clearly to them both who was in charge.

Without another word, Kellerman turned sharply and strode towards the van.

#   #   #

Elmer Dobbs applied the brakes, stopping his truck just outside the entrance to Lot 4 of Tomahawk Woods. A sawhorse with a sign hanging off it blocked the driveway.

"What is that?" Dan Butler asked, squinting through the front windshield to see the sign.

In bold, hand-written letters, the sign read "CLOSED." Along with it, yellow police tape hung all over the lot, blocking the entrance to the main trail leading into the woods.

"How do you close a forest?" Dan wondered, but Elmer was already climbing out of the truck.

As Dan watched, Elmer walked over to the sawhorse, picked it up, and moved it out of the way. Then he climbed back into the cab and started to put the truck back into gear, but Dan stopped him.

"Wait," Dan said, a bit of uncertainty in his voice.

Elmer looked over at him but didn't say anything. Dan waited a moment, hesitant to ask. But after Elmer's story, a sleepless night, and the increasing strangeness of the whole situation, he decided he needed to.

"Do you have another gun I can have?"

Elmer raised an eyebrow, surprised at the request. He didn't think Dan had it in him. But still without a word, Elmer reached across Dan's lap and opened the glove compartment. When his hand emerged, he was holding a black handgun with a long barrel and thick handle grip.

"You know how to use one of these?" Elmer finally spoke, holding the gun out for Dan to take.

"I've shot a gun before," Dan answered, sounding like he was trying to convince himself more than Elmer.

"This here's a KelTec PMR-30," Elmer answered, as if any of that alphabet soup would mean anything to Dan. "Take it."

Dan hesitated again, but finally reached for the weapon and held it in his hand. It was lighter than he would have expected.

"It's easy to shoot, an' it don't have much kick," Elmer went on. "It's still dangerous. Give it respect."

"What are the odds I'm going to have to use this thing?" Dan asked, already second-guessing his decision to ask for the firearm.

Elmer stared at him.

"Just stick it in your pocket," he said, "and don't shoot me."

With that, Elmer pulled into the lot and parked.

#   #   #

Chief Donovan opened the holding cell, still bristling over the way that the mayor and his strange new colleagues were ordering him around. In particular—though he deep down relished making Emmaline cool her heels in his jail for a night—the idea of detaining a reporter for digging through city files was admittedly ridiculous. And eventually Donovan himself would likely face some sort of accountability for it, he knew.

Opening the holding cell, Donovan stepped inside with a rag and cleaning spray. With the Jubilee kicking off, it was likely that he'd be dealing with at least a couple drunk and disorderly's before too long. *And who else but the goddamn Chief of Police should wipe down the cell?* he thought. Not to mention the fact that Emmaline had angrily informed him on the way out that morning that she had left him a "present" inside. *God only knows what that means*, he thought as he sprayed and wiped down the bench, his eyes darting around to find whatever unpleasantness she had left behind.

Letting his mind wander, Donovan pondered what Mayor Cankerby might be up to. He didn't believe Jackson's crazy monster-in-the-woods story for a minute. But something clearly was going on that could pose a significant danger to the residents of Tomahawk Hollow. The most likely scenario, he still believed, was a rogue wolf or bobcat that was acting erratically. He still hadn't come up with any answers to explain the disappearance of the tourist Wilson, though. And even though the mayor had insisted that he'd spoken with Jake Madsen yesterday, Donovan didn't believe him. It concerned him that he'd been unable to contact Jake or Claire himself, and he was determined to make one more trip out to the Madsen farm before the Jubilee got into full swing.

Making matters worse, this mysterious "private security team" had showed up out of nowhere, and Cankerby was refusing to tell Donovan where they had come from or who was footing the bill. The mayor had simply insisted that they were there to deal with the slaughtered livestock situation and to help ensure the safety of the Jubilee. And Cankerby also made it clear that Donovan required no further information than that. It was as if the chief—

Donovan stopped what he was doing.

Close to the metal bench that he was wiping down, something caught his eye that he couldn't remember seeing before. It appeared to be writing scratched into the wall.

Moving closer to inspect it, Donovan spotted a beat-up old penny lying on the floor. Its rough and jagged edges suggested it had been used to scrawl the markings into the painted brick. Donovan crouched down to get a better look and noted that the writing consisted of two words, which—taken together—meant nothing to him.

Blutmond Holdings.

Chapter 24

AS THEIR INSCRUTABLE ESCORTS USHERED Jackson and Emmaline out of the van, the two journalists took in the strange scene around them. To get the vehicle into Lot 3, the man who called himself Kellerman had directed one of his lackeys to temporarily remove a barrier that was blocking the entrance. They had then pulled into the lot, which was roped off on all sides with yellow police tape.

Without saying anything, Jackson noted that the lot was empty: the BMW Series 5 sedan he'd seen the other day was gone.

Kellerman directed the process of unloading equipment from the van. He and his underlings—they still hadn't spoken a single word between them, so Jackson had dubbed them Blondie and Bug Eyes—busied themselves preparing various packs and weapons for their operation. Jackson watched with particular concern as Blondie strapped a flamethrower to his back and Bug Eyes placed several olive-green blocks of what might have passed for puddy or clay into a backpack. The blocks were bound together with blue electrical tape, wires connecting them to a compact detonator with a digital display screen.

"C4?" Jackson blurted out. "One's got a flamethrower and the other's loading C4 into a backpack? What the hell's going to happen out there?"

"Mr. Reed," Kellerman responded, "before we proceed into the forest, I will need you to turn over your cell phone."

Kellerman's demand caught Jackson off guard. "What?"

"Per our agreement," the intimidating soldier stood in front of Jackson, "you may keep your camera and your recording device; and you may report on everything that you see today. However, I will not allow you to interfere in any way with the execution of this dangerous mission. That includes communicating with the outside world before we have completed our task. For that reason, I am going to take and hold onto your phone until that time."

Emmaline and Jackson exchanged looks, both recognizing the vulnerable position that would put them in.

"There's no way I'm giving you my phone," Jackson scoffed, but—still rattled by the heavy weaponry the soldiers were preparing for their expedition—it didn't come out nearly as assertive as he wanted it to.

Once again, Kellerman's lips curled into a humorless sneer as he stepped forward. "Mr. Reed," Kellerman growled, "please understand that nothing that happens from now until we emerge from these woods is subject to negotiation."

Both Emmaline and Jackson noted with some surprise that Kellerman's words were no longer tinged with that awkward faux-American accent. Instead, his voice filled with guttural German inflections.

"There will be no conversations, discussions, or debates. We are entering into an uncertain, potentially treacherous scenario. I will not tolerate anything that puts myself, my men, or my mission in jeopardy. Do you understand?" Kellerman's fingers fanned out and quickly tapped themselves over his sidearm one at a time.

"Hand me your cell phone, Mr. Reed. Right now."

Convinced that any further objection would be fruitless—and would potentially endanger both him and Emmaline—Jackson reached into his pocket and pulled out his phone.

"Thank you, Mr. Reed," Kellerman hissed. He plucked the phone away from Jackson, turned, and walked over to Blondie, handing it to him. "Now, shall we into the woods?"

Pocketing the phone, Blondie heaved a large duffle bag up, slung it over his shoulder, and strode toward the main trail into Tomahawk Woods. Kellerman extended an arm toward the path, directing Jackson and Emmaline to follow Blondie.

They did.

With Blondie several paces ahead of them and Kellerman and Bug Eyes several paces behind, Jackson and Emmaline ducked under the police tape. Once on the path, Emmaline glanced at their attendants ahead and behind them to be sure they couldn't hear her.

"He didn't demand *my* phone," Emmaline whispered to Jackson.

"I thought you didn't know where it was?" Jackson questioned.

"I don't," Emmaline replied, glancing back at Kellerman, "but he obviously does."

Chapter 25

DAN BUTLER AND ELMER DOBBS stopped.

Now a few hours into their third day searching these woods, they were following a lesser-traveled branch off one of the main hiking trails. But what they now saw forty yards ahead stopped them in their tracks.

"I'll be damned," Elmer mumbled, remembering for the first time in years the old cabin that he and his friends used to frequent when they were kids.

As youngsters, they would play there while their dads were out hunting or fishing nearby. As teenagers they'd sneak out to the isolated shack to drink and carouse with girls from school. Even back the first time he saw it, though, the nondescript shelter was already abandoned and beginning its descent into disrepair. Now, decades later, sitting there in a large clearing in the woods, it was still structurally intact…but age and decay were more than having their way with it.

Near the shack, an elevated hunting blind rose from the dirt and grass some ten feet off the ground. Though clearly not as old as the cabin itself, the hand-built blind had also seen better days. The weathered wooden planks of its rickety support structure exhibited the bruises and scars of countless unforgiving seasons. A short ladder—moss and lichen drooping from its rotting rungs—climbed to the entrance of the enclosed platform. Higher up, two shooting windows suggested sunken, weary eyes on an expressionless face.

"What is it?" Dan asked.

"An old hunters shack," Elmer told him. "Been out here as long as I can remember. I ain't seen it or even thought about it for twenty years, though."

Elmer took a step towards the rundown old cabin, but Dan grabbed him.

"Hold on there. Whose is it?"

"I don't know," Elmer shrugged. "Nobody's, maybe. Not now, at least."

Elmer pulled away and continued forward.

With Dan watching from behind, Elmer approached the rotting old shack. It seemed to grow out of a sea of overgrown weeds and brush all around the clearing. Like the blind, years of relentless summer rains and winter snow had left it with a sickly gray pallor. A single window was shattered—a few fragments of glass still jutted out of the rotting frame—but it appeared boarded up from the inside with considerably younger wood.

A thick, distinctive smell slowed Elmer's approach.

Part of it was that familiar pungent odor that hung in the air at local filling stations and the small machine shops where Elmer sometimes worked.

Gasoline.

But blended with it was something far more foul and nauseating. Something entirely unfamiliar to Elmer.

At first he thought it was just the pervasive odor of decay hanging heavy in the air, a musty mix of damp wood, mold, and forgotten memories. But the closer he got, the more repugnant the stench became. With every step, the noxious, fetid bouquet pushed at him, churning his stomach and threatening to trigger a violent expulsion of the contents of his stomach.

From behind, Dan could see Elmer slow down, and for a moment he thought he saw his companion become unsteady on his feet. Beginning to inhale the first hints of the acrid stank now himself, Dan called out, "Are you okay, Elmer?"

Elmer raised his hand.

"Stay there," he commanded with a suddenly weak voice, having spotted something that now filled him with dread.

It sat near the hunting blind, mostly hidden by a canvas tarp draped over it. But a thick tire was just visible in the gap between the tarp and the ground, and Elmer immediately recognized it as an ATV.

His ATV.

The one Dave had borrowed three days ago for his camping trip.

The realization stopped him momentarily but then quickly propelled him forward, unnerved and urgent. Deep down he knew that after days of searching for his son, he literally was on the doorstep of an answer.

Elmer placed a hand on the door of the shack, giving it a shove and letting it swing inwards on its rusty hinges. As soon as it opened, a chunky, sour bile rose from Elmer's stomach, caught the tobacco in his mouth, and bubbled through his lips down onto the doorstep. Wobbling, Elmer braced himself against the doorframe. Even as he willed himself to stay on his feet, a second cascade of vomitous retch exploded from his mouth and splashed to the ground.

"Elmer!" Dan cried, seeing the other's distress.

Dan started forward, but Elmer called out sharply again.

"Stay there!" he repeated, this time forcefully.

Dan froze on the path.

Struggling to force down a third wave of spew, Elmer's wide eyes took in the horrifying scene of carnage and death inside the hunters' shack.

The small shelter was no more than fifteen feet wide by ten feet deep. Elmer could now see that the wood planks covering its one window were clean and devoid of rot, unlike the rest of the structure. And though there was no furniture or equipment of any kind inside, the cabin was far from empty.

Everywhere that Elmer looked, bloody, butchered corpses lay strewn and stacked on the rotting wooden floor. Just past the bilious regurgitation at his feet, what once must have been a middle-aged man had somehow been reduced to a broken, twisted mess of shattered bones and shredded flesh. His chest was ripped open and what remained of his left leg ended in a bloody stump. The foot that should have been attached to it rested on its side a few feet away.

Just beyond the man's corpse lay the carcasses of two deer—one might have been the same one that he and Dan had found the other day—and a large wolf. All of them had been similarly slaughtered.

Scattered around the floor were random severed limbs and disemboweled entrails. Elmer couldn't distinguish at first glance if the organs and viscera were from man or animal. But even more horrifying, at the far end of the cabin, a grotesque pile of mangled and mutilated carcasses and corpses rose from the floor.

Some were cattle and livestock, and some were woodland creatures. Others were people. Elmer knew everyone in Tomahawk Hollow, and while he didn't recognize the middle-aged man directly in front of him, he realized with another stomach-churning jolt that it was the remains of Claire and Jake Madsen resting atop the bloody assemblage across the cabin.

And the gory waste and wreckage all around him appeared to be soaked not just with blood but with gasoline, as well.

Elmer's eyes scanned frantically over the mound of slaughtered flesh and stopped suddenly when he saw it. A thin female arm jutted randomly out of the pile with delicate, pretty painted nails. Though he couldn't see the rest of her, a silver charm bracelet hung off her wrist, and Elmer recognized it immediately. He had given it to his wife, Clara, the year before she'd been diagnosed with colon cancer. And shortly before she had succumbed, Clara had passed it on to Dave, urging him to give it to a young woman who reminded him of her.

Elmer knew that it was Dan's daughter, Cheri, wearing that bracelet.

And that meant that somewhere in that pile was his own son, Dave.

Elmer's face flushed red, and for the first time since his wife passed he felt a hot sting in his eyes. Elmer swallowed hard, trying desperately to suppress the sob that was about to rise out of him.

Then Dan called out again from behind, "Elmer!"

Elmer's voice croaked, almost breaking as he repeated one more time, "Stay there!"

But this time Dan sounded neither hesitant nor uncertain when he cried out again, "ELMER!"

Elmer turned.

If the scene inside the cabin sickened him, the scene outside nearly snapped his mind.

As Dan stumbled backwards towards the cabin in terror, two grotesque monstrosities—each with bloated, mottled bodies bigger than full-grown boars—burst out of the woods with remarkable speed. Their spindly legs kicked up a furious storm of leaves and sticks as they pounded the earth in pursuit of their prey.

In his awkward retreat, Dan's feet tangled. He pitched backwards, crashing to the ground with a hard thump. The giant ticks closed quickly on the fallen man, their palps twitching in an excited frenzy.

In a delirium of terror, Dan tried to scramble back, kicking furiously and madly punching the heels of his hands at the ground. The closest tick was nearly on him, though, rising slightly on its hind legs as if gloating over its prey. Its harpoon-like hypostome extended from its mouthparts like a hideous, barbed erection.

Dan unleashed a desperate, pleading cry for help, but a deafening roar behind him drowned it out. A cascade of chitin exploded off the hard scutum of the tick and sent it stumbling backwards.

When Dan looked behind him, he saw Elmer standing in the cabin doorway with a Magnum Research Desert Eagle gripped in both hands.

Eyes wide and mouth agape, Elmer watched the unimaginable abomination he just shot rattle and rage violently. Despite his utter shock, he squeezed the trigger again, and another thunderous boom filled the air. As he fired over and over, the torrent of blistering gunfire sent a barrage of heavy bullets slamming into the monstrous tick like thunderbolts and pushed it backwards.

Recognizing this new threat, the other tick abandoned its pursuit of Dan and altered course. Setting its sights on Elmer, it scuttled past Dan and raced toward the man in the cabin doorway.

Elmer redirected his aim and leveled the hand cannon at the charging monster. Three quick rounds exploded from the barrel, hammering into its scutum and unleashing a shower of putrid ichor and chitin shards. The beast writhed and screeched in agonized fury, momentarily halted by the power of the weapon.

With the creature stunned, Elmer squeezed the trigger again, but this time the gun clicked impotently. He had exhausted his ammunition.

Ejecting the empty cartridge to the ground, Elmer reached a shaking hand into his jacket pocket for a new one. Fumbling to snap it into place, he called out to Dan.

"Shoot it!" Elmer cried. "Shoot it!"

His mind still reeling from the unthinkable horror of the last sixty seconds, Dan had his wits enough to reach his own trembling hand into the pocket of his windbreaker. It emerged gripping the KelTec pistol Elmer had given him in the truck. Dan felt around quickly for the safety and released it.

Positioned between him and Elmer, the giant tick was recovered enough from the force of Elmer's attack to prepare a second assault. With its front legs waving their razor-sharp claws, it advanced on Elmer, who was still reloading his weapon.

"Shoot it!" Elmer cried again.

Still on the ground, Dan sat up enough to grip the KelTec with both hands and raise it towards the tick. Holding his breath, he began to fire.

With little recoil behind each round, Dan squeezed the trigger repeatedly. The KelTec barked out angrily with each successive shot. The tick's hard scutum extended only over the front two-thirds of its body, leaving its swollen rear soft and unprotected from the hail of gunfire. As the 9mm rounds ripped into its exposed idiosoma, they unleashed explosive geysers of putrid bile. Penetrating into the beast's inner body, the unrelenting barrage exploded its rectal sac first, then its salivary glands. And as the creature screamed and shuddered under the attack, the gunfire tore through and mangled its tracheal tubes.

Twelve shots into his assault, Dan's arms began to weaken. With his aim faltering, the bullets started kicking up dirt and leaves as they slammed into the ground. Behind the tick, a stray shot tore into Elmer's thigh. Blood splattered from the wound, and he collapsed to the ground.

Seeing Elmer fall, Dan ceased firing, mortified to realize he'd shot his companion. But even as Elmer writhed on the ground in pain, Dan could see that the mutant tick between them wasn't moving anymore, and its inhuman screeching had gone silent.

Remembering then that the now-dead monster was not alone, Dan spun in the dirt and raised the handgun again. He waved it around, struggling to get eyes on the creature. But it was nowhere to be found, apparently chased off by the unexpected violence that had been inflicted upon it and its fellow mutant.

Then Dan twisted himself around again, trying to catch his breath there on the ground. Beyond the tick's carcass, he could hear Elmer gasping and cursing in pain.

"Are you alright?" Dan called over, beginning to force himself to his feet.

"No, goddamnit!" Elmer cursed again. "I told you not to shoot me!"

Chapter 26

THE HUNTING PARTY HALTED WHEN they heard the first gunshots in the distance. One short burst and then another, followed by a bestial shriek. Emmaline shuddered and looked over at Jackson. Something about his grim expression told her that he had heard the sound before.

"What is that?"

Kellerman raised a hand sharply and hissed an emphatic, "Shhhhhhh!"

They all froze on the path, trying to identify the direction from which the sounds were coming.

A moment later, more gunfire crackled in the distance, followed by another grotesque screech. The German mercenary directed his gaze toward the remote, unseen melee. It was coming from the same direction in which they'd been headed. In silence, the group waited for more commotion, but after several moments it was over.

Scowling, Kellerman shook his head.

The high-power walkie-talkie hanging from Blondie's belt emitted an echo-y voice, "Basis an Kommandant. Basis an Kommandant."

Blondie handed the device to Kellerman, who took it and spoke.

"Hier ist Kellermann. Was ist los?"

"Wir haben Zugriff auf das Mobiltelefon," the voice answered back.

Kellerman glanced over at Emaline and Jackson, who were watching him closely.

"Warte einen Moment," Kellerman said. Then he walked far enough down the path so that the conversation could not be heard.

As Emmaline and Jackson watched him, Kellerman nodded occasionally and once cocked his head to look back in their direction. The longer the conversation went, the more agitated the normally inscrutable German seemed. At one point, he began punctuating his orders by stabbing a finger forward, as if jabbing it into the chest of a cowering underling.

When he finished, Kellerman walked back towards the group. He handed the walkie-talkie back to Blondie and strode right up to Emmaline. He hovered over her, looking down through his dark glasses.

"Aren't you clever," he snarled. Emmaline didn't understand.

Jackson looked from one to the other. "What's going on?"

Kellerman slowly craned his head to glare at Jackson. Then, just as deliberately, he turned back to focus intently on Emmaline.

"I'm pleased to inform you, Miss Blackdeer," he began, "that your lost cellular phone has been found. And to ensure that you not miss any important messages, my colleague penetrated its security protocols to access your email."

He paused to see if she would respond.

She didn't.

"Congratulations on capturing those truly remarkable photos. Unfortunately, in doing so you have severely compromised my ability to contain this unfortunate situation…and at the same time brought an end to the charade of this expedition."

"Enough riddles, Kellerman," Jackson insisted. "What the hell are you talking about?"

"What I'm talking about, Mr. Reed," Kellerman answered, glowering, "is the official dissolution of our arrangement. Miss Blackdeer has seen to that."

Jackson opened his mouth to respond but paused. He understood from the sudden escalation of tension that their peril had increased dramatically. Grabbing Emmaline by the arm, Jackson pulled her away from Kellerman.

"Then we're done here," Jackson huffed, trying to sound authoritative as he and Emmaline began to retreat back in the direction from which they had come.

Without hesitation, Kellerman's men unholstered their handguns and leveled them at the two journalists. Jackson and Emmaline stopped.

"Kellerman—" Jackson began but was immediately cut off.

"SHUT UP!" Kellerman bellowed, the explosion of emotion causing Jackson and Emmaline to flinch. Just as quickly, the German composed himself, resuming the mocking, amused tone that he so often employed.

"Really, Mr. Reed," he taunted, "were we not all ready to dispense with this pointless deception, in any event? I cannot imagine that you believed you would ever actually cash that check in your desk drawer, did you?"

Surprised, Emmaline shot Jackson a look, but after meeting her eyes for the briefest moment, Jackson looked away. Whether it was from the overwhelming feeling of foolishness or shame, he didn't know, but Jackson couldn't maintain eye contact with his protégé.

"Now that we all understand each other," Kellerman continued, "allow me to put this as plainly as I can. We would be happy to shoot you right now if that is your wish. But that would require us to drag your lifeless bodies the rest of the way to our destination, which—admittedly—would be both inconvenient and increase our vulnerability to the threats in these woods. Alternatively, we can continue on our way and engage in those inevitable unpleasantries when we reach our destination. In my humble opinion, the latter option is the mutually preferable one."

Both Jackson and Emmaline were speechless at the sinister intention behind Kellerman's equally dire options.

"Seeing, then, that neither of you has expressed a preference," Kellerman sneered, "I propose that we adopt the latter option until such time as either of you do something rash that forces my men to accelerate your termination. Are we agreed?"

Again, Emmaline and Jackson were stunned, though Emmaline attempted to weakly object to Kellerman's threat.

"You can't seriously think you can just murder us?" she protested. "People know you took us out here. The mayor, Tim—"

Kellerman raised a finger to his lips and hissed back at Emmaline, "Shhhh."

The sheer force of his will silenced her.

He stepped forward to hover over her once more.

"Please cease your pointless prattle, Miss Blackdeer," Kellerman growled. "At this point in time, the only thing I want to hear from you is the answer to this one simple question: Who is Dr. Alena Sokolová?"

Chapter 27

CHIEF DONOVAN CLIMBED OUT OF his black and white SUV, slammed the door shut, and surveyed the Madsen property. Nothing seemed out of the ordinary, so he went to the back door. Leaning to look through the window into the kitchen, he pressed the buzzer and waited for an answer.

None came.

"Jake!" he called out.

The only answer was the staccato ring of his cell phone.

Fishing the phone out of his pocket, Donovan looked at the screen. A long twelve-digit phone number came up, starting with +420. Below the number was the image of an unfamiliar flag: a white rectangle on top of a red rectangle with a blue triangle laid over them.

Donovan was annoyed. It was the third call he had received from this number since he left the station, and he was in no mood to deal with a telemarketing scam at the moment. He denied the call and pocketed the phone.

"Claire!" he said loudly, now banging a fist against the door. "It's Chief Donovan! Please open up!"

Again, no answer, so Donovan let his eyes scan back over the property. From the barn…over their beat-up powder-blue pickup truck…past the silo… and into the soy field with the big yellow tractor parked nearby.

Then it struck him.

If they've gone away like Cankerby said, Donovan thought, *why's the truck still there?*

He strained to remember if they had another vehicle but couldn't picture one. Besides, things were tight for most farm families in Tomahawk Hollow, making a second car a luxury. And Jake and Claire Madsen weren't exactly luxury people.

He tried turning the doorknob but found it locked.

Donovan sighed. In the urban jungle where he came up as a cop, things were almost always what they seemed. When he got a call for domestic battery, a bruised and bloody woman always answered the door. When he responded to a robbery in progress, the perp running from the scene was the one who did it. When a gangbanger turned up dead, the rival gang was responsible. That's just how it worked.

But here, nothing was out of the ordinary…and yet everything seemed wrong.

Pulling his nightstick off his belt, Donovan glanced around one more time. Then, with a flick of his wrist, he shattered one of the small windowpanes in the backdoor. Knocking the remaining shards away with the hardwood stick, Donovan reached in carefully and turned the lock. A moment later, he was inside the Madsen's kitchen and closing the door behind him.

The first thing that Donovan noticed was an absence. He had only been inside the Madsen's home twice before, and both times the mouthwatering smells of freshly baked breads and other sweet treats had filled the kitchen. Today he detected only the faint scent of the flower bouquet decorating the center of the kitchen table. That seemed to confirm that Claire Madsen, at least, had not been there for at least a day.

All around him the house was quiet. When Donovan took the couple of steps from the kitchen into the living room, the slight creaking of the floorboards filled both rooms.

As he moved his patrol from one room to the next, he noted a collection of family photos adorning the walls and the mantle of a small fireplace. Kids and grandkids. Family vacations. And one multi-generational family photo that included more family members than Donovan cared to count.

Golden afternoon sun poured in through the large picture window that overlooked the front porch and yard, brightening the entire living room. As Donovan scanned his eyes around, a shimmer on the floor caught his eye. Bending down, he retrieved a slender, inch-long shard of clear, broken glass. He would never have seen it, he guessed, had the bright sun not caught it and made it dance with light. Donovan turned it over in his hands, glancing around to see if any of the glass in the photo frames appeared cracked or broken. None seemed to be.

Placing the sliver on an end table, Donovan turned towards the staircase and began the climb to the second floor. Despite the order and tranquility of the quaint farmhouse, he continued to feel uneasy.

At the top of the stairs, Donovan found his way to the master bedroom. Just as he was about to enter, his cell phone began to ring and vibrate again.

"Goddammit," he mumbled under his breath, pulling out the phone. Sure enough, it was the same +420 number and strange flag. Donovan had had enough.

Alright, asshole, he thought, *let's go.*

"Before you say a word," Donovan answered angrily, "I want you to know that this is the Chief of Police of Tomahawk Hollow, Wisconsin. And I have the ability to forensically trace the exact origin of this call." He didn't, actually. "Now, who the hell are you and why have you been calling me over and over for the past half hour?"

There was a pause on the other end of the line, the caller clearly caught off guard. Donovan smiled, pleased, but then a woman with a thick accent answered.

"Chief Donovan?" she asked. "My name is Dr. Alena Sokolová, and I'm sorry to have been so insistent with my calls." She paused, waiting for a response, but this time it was Donovan who was caught a bit off guard. "You see," she continued, "I received a series of highly disturbing photos from Emmaline Blackdeer, and I wasn't sure how to…do you know Miss Blackdeer?"

"Yeah, I know Em," Donovan confirmed. "What photos?"

"Well, that's the thing," Dr. Sokolová continued, "she emailed me these photos that seem to depict…well, they're very graphic, and if they are real, I thought that local law enforcement should be made aware. I've tried to contact Miss Blackdeer, but she hasn't responded." She paused again. "Would it be alright to switch to video call, please?"

"Okay," Donovan muttered, and she sent him an invitation to chat by video. The two of them were now face to face, and Donovan could see that the mysterious caller appeared nervous but sincere.

"Thank you," she told him. "I think that you should take a look at these."

Dr. Sokolová flipped her camera and then focused the frame on a laptop computer. Its screen was sleeping, so she jiggled the mouse, bringing the image on the laptop to life.

Seeing it gave Donovan chills.

Claire Madsen lay on the ground, broken and bloody and torn clean open. Before he could react, Dr. Sokolová clicked the laptop, and the image shifted to another angle on Claire's corpse, this one more clearly demonstrating the diminishment of her body from extreme blood loss. Another click and Donovan caught his breath, seeing a similarly slaughtered Jake Madsen. His body was partially hidden among the soy plants, but he had clearly been treated to the same horrific brutality as his wife of forty-some years.

The doctor clicked through a few more photos. Two more angles on Jake. The old man's severed arm from the elbow down laying in the soy field. A wide shot of the field with the shuttered pesticide plant in the distance behind it. And two shattered windows, one that looked like it led to the Madsen's kitchen and the other that was on the second floor. Donovan looked over the intact window in the bedroom he was standing in. It may have been that one.

Dr. Sokolová flipped her camera again so that Donovan could see her.

"So you see," she went on, "why I'm concerned."

Still holding the phone, Donovan struggled with his other hand to extract a cigarette from the pack in his pocket, pop it into his mouth, and find his lighter. Jostling his cell phone around as he did, he finally spoke, the cigarette bobbing in his mouth, "Who are you again?"

Understanding that it would take him a moment to get his arms around what she had shown him, Dr. Sokolová spoke patiently.

"My name is Dr. Alena Sokolová," she repeated. "I'm an acarology researcher at the Institute of Parasitology in Branišovská in the Czech Republic."

"I don't…" Donovan began, but then asked more directly, "What is *aracology?*"

"*Acarology,*" she corrected, "is a subfield of the broader discipline of arachnology, which is the study of arachnids, a class of joint-legged invertebrates that includes spiders, scorpions, etc."

"Uh huh." By now Donovan had lit his cigarette and was inhaling a long first drag.

"In my specific subdiscipline," she continued, "we examine the taxonomy, anatomy, physiology, behavior, ecology, and ecosystem functions of certain tiny members of the subclass Acari within the class Arachnida, including mites…" She paused for just a moment.

"Look, doctor—"

"…and ticks."

The word came out like a piece of bait hooked to the end of a fishing line. She watched him to see if he would snatch it.

Donovan expelled the smoke from his drag forcefully.

"'Ticks'?" he repeated, as if he possibly could have misunderstood the word.

"Yes, Chief Donovan," Dr. Sokolová replied, fascinated by his reaction. "Does that mean something to you?"

Realizing that he had just filled the Madsen's bedroom with smoke, Donovan walked over to the window and pushed it open to ventilate the room.

"Why should it?" he asked carefully, not wanting to show his hand to this stranger. He sat down on the bed next to the open window and took another drag, careful to blow the smoke outside.

"Well, you see," she explained, "when I first spoke with Miss Blackdeer, she and her associate were inquiring with relation to an extraordinary story that they shared with me. Of course, I didn't believe it, but after seeing these photos, I do believe that they have discovered something dangerous in or around your town."

Drawing again from the cigarette, Donovan tried to chemically calm himself down. Without exhaling, he probed further, though he already knew the answer. "What story?"

He leaned toward the window again and blew out the smoke.

"It seems," she answered, almost embarrassed by what she was about to convey, "that Miss Blackdeer's colleague believes that he came across—"

Dr. Sokolová stopped talking. She could see that Donovan was no longer looking at his phone screen, but instead was staring out the window next to him. His stunned expression was enough to stop her mid-sentence.

"Chief Donovan? What's wrong?"

Chapter 28

"I'M SORRY."

It had taken Jackson quite some time to say anything at all to Emmaline as they trudged along a seldom-traveled trail through Tomahawk Woods. Whatever they had previously thought the outcome of this excursion might be was long forgotten. Both were now grimly aware that they were on a quintessential death march. And not knowing how far it was to their destination, they had no idea how long they had before they reached the end of the line. So even though Jackson knew those two words were inadequate, they were all he'd been able to come up with.

Emmaline eyed Jackson resentfully. She certainly wasn't blameless for their current predicament, she thought. She should have never let the mayor march her to jail like that. Maybe she had just let her trust in Jackson cloud her judgement. And now it seemed likely that it would be the last mistake she'd ever make.

"What was the deal?" she challenged in a low voice.

"What?" It's not that Jackson didn't understand the question so much as he was buying time to come up with a better answer.

"Jackson," she scolded, "you didn't put our lives at risk out here with these psychotic storm troopers just to get a good story. What was the real deal?"

Jackson exhaled deeply, glancing at the men who were now clearly their captors. Bug Eyes was leading their march, hands gripping a heavy rifle and eyes darting warily from side to side. Behind him and Emmaline walked Blondie, his concentration similarly engaged on detecting any sign of danger in the trees. And bringing up the rear—quite a way back—followed Kellerman, who was engaged in a low-toned discussion on the walkie-talkie he'd taken back again.

"Money," Jackson admitted, embarrassed. "They paid me off."

Emmaline shook her head.

"You have no idea the hole I'm in," Jackson snapped. "Every month, I lose more money. Every day my debt gets bigger. And all I have to show for it is a failing business in a moribund industry serving a community that— once people actually learn what's been happening here—will shrivel up and die itself. And then what? I'm fifty-three years old, buried in dept that I can never pay off...living hand-to-mouth? No. That's not fair. They said they'd take this rotting carcass of a newspaper off my hands, cancel my debts, and send me off with a check for one million dollars."

Jackson glared at Emmaline, waiting for a response.

"Did you hear me, Em? A million dollars. How was I supposed to say no to that?"

"For God's sake, Jackson," Emmaline fumed, partially out of anger and partially out of pity, "you're a newspaper man! You're supposed to recognize when a story is too good to be true!"

Jackson looked away, knowing she was right.

"There's no money," she continued, "no magic wand that's going to make all your troubles disappear…and certainly no deal with these thugs!"

She glanced back at Bug Eyes and then lowered her voice even further. "They're going to kill you."

Jackson snorted. "So? What the hell do I have to live for at this point?"

"That's fine for you, Jackson," Emmaline snapped, "but they're going to kill me, too!"

Jackson flushed hot with shame. He knew she was right, and he knew it was his fault.

"Dear God, Em, I'm so, so sorry," he repeated, but somehow it meant even less now than when he first said it.

Chapter 29

GAWKING OUT THE WINDOW OF the Madsens' bedroom, Chief Donovan had no idea how to respond to Dr. Sokolová. From his vantage point from the second floor, he could see it moving from the direction of the barn and towards the soy field. And it absolutely was not any farm animal he had ever seen before.

It was difficult to determine the exact size, but the extraordinary creature below him had an oval brown body with six crooked black limbs carrying it along over the ground. Though Donovan could determine no head or face, two stubby protrusions extended out from where a head might have been—assuming solely based on the direction it was moving and the general shape of its anatomy—and they separated and closed repeatedly as it moved.

Donovan had seen more than his share of shocking and disturbing things since he first took his oath to protect and serve, but none of them had been in Tomahawk Hollow. And none of them came close to matching the unimaginable monstrosity he was looking at now.

"Chief?" Dr. Sokolová pressed. "What's wrong?"

"It's…" Donovan croaked, but his mouth had gone so dry it was hard to speak. Unable to say the word, he fumbled with his phone, flipping the camera and pointing it toward the thing in the yard.

At first the image was too distant to see it clearly, but Donovan zoomed the camera in. As the image came into focus, Dr. Sokolová gasped. Though she, too, doubted her own eyes, she certainly recognized an *Ixodes scapularis* when she saw it.

A black legged tick.

A giant one.

With the camera following the creature along, the mutant tick passed in front of the Madsens' pickup truck. It stopped for just a moment, giving Donovan and the Czech researcher a chilling sense of the scale and size of the monster. From front to rear, its length looked to be about the same as the diameter of one of the truck's tires. And though its width did not match its length, the extension of its six legs from side to side gave it a disconcerting appearance of aberrant physical brawn.

"Dear God," she breathed. "Is that real?"

"I'm seeing it just like you are," Donovan sputtered.

As they continued to watch, the thing resumed its journey. With each step it took, the clawed ends of its long legs dug into the ground and propelled it along. When it reached the edge of the soy field, it disappeared among the plants, the only evidence left of its migration the rustling of vegetation as it went.

Donovan continued to train the phone's camera on the tick's path until its movement through the field was no longer perceptible. Dr. Sokolová's voice snapped him out of his stunned stupor.

"That's the most extraordinary thing I've ever seen," she marveled as Donovan readjusted the camera so that they could both see each other again. "Please say that you recorded that."

Embarrassed that he hadn't even thought to do so, Donovan ignored the comment.

"That was a tick, right?" he stammered, though it couldn't possibly have been anything else.

"Based on its shape and color, as well as the presence of the hard scutum shielding its upper dorsal region," she explained, "that was what would normally be known as a black-legged tick, or a common deer tick."

"Common?" Donovan snorted.

"Well," she admitted, "the dimensions are unlike anything that has ever been known to exist before. I must say—though I would not have imagined it to be the case before—I would say that the violence depicted in those photos that Miss Blackdeer sent me would certainly be consistent with what a tick of such substantial…*proportions*…could inflict."

That mention of Emmaline's name triggered something in Donovan's mind.

"Does the name Blutmond Holdings mean anything to you?"

"Blutmond Holdings?" she repeated, caught off guard by the question. "Of course. Why on earth would you ask that?"

"What is it?" Donovan pressed.

"They're a rather disreputable biochemical and biotechnology concern with German roots," she explained. "More of a rogue actor than a legitimate corporation, though that is the façade they maintain. Blutmond has been heavily sanctioned by the European Union for unethical and illegal research and development. And its security division has come under heavy scrutiny for alleged extralegal activities, including bribery and coercion, as well as various other nefarious schemes. As you might imagine, they are rather notorious in the scientific community, particularly on this side of the Atlantic Ocean."

"I don't understand. What kind of research?"

"If I recall correctly, they have had their fingers in any number of pies," Dr. Sokolová continued. "They have been known to establish foreign subsidiaries that are difficult to trace back to Blutmond, which they use to pursue banned or prohibited R&D under the guise of developing and manufacturing legitimate biochemical products. I believe they've previously been sanctioned for illicit efforts related to biochemical weapons, clandestine animal testing, synthetic—"

Dr. Sokolová stopped, realizing immediately that she was about to articulate the answer.

"Synthetic what?" Donovan asked.

"Growth hormones," she finished. "Synthetic growth hormones."

For several moments, neither said anything, both processing not just what they saw, but also the implications of the answer they seemed to have stumbled upon. And then Donovan put the final piece into place.

"Could one of those false-front businesses be a pesticide plant?" he asked, though to him the answer now seemed obvious.

"Certainly," she responded. "From what I know of their history, that would be right in line with the Blutmond modus operandi."

Donovan shook his head and looked back out the bedroom window, across the field, and to the shuttered building beyond it.

"Then I know where this thing came from," Donovan declared, "and I know where it's going right now. If I can get over there, I—" He paused, rolling his eyes. "I can't believe I'm saying this. But if I can get over there now, I should be able to take it out before it causes any further damage."

Dr. Sokolová made no attempt to disguise her skepticism.

"Chief Donovan, it's possible that whatever it was that produced this phenomenal physical mutation could also have produced marked changes to a standard tick's behavior or temperament."

"Temperament?"

"Well," she laughed a single chuckle at herself, "for lack of a better word. My point, though, is that some synthetic growth hormones have been known to increase aggression in their subjects. According to Miss Blackdeer and Mr. Reed, they have already observed that increased aggression first-hand. And that's just one potential side effect. I fear that there could be others, as well. What I'm saying is that it is very possible that you are facing an extremely dangerous, unpredictable situation."

"I think we've already established that," Donovan noted wryly, recalling not just the Madsen photos but also the slaughtered livestock he'd seen earlier in the week.

"But that's not all," Dr. Sokolová said. "You suggested that you'd be able to 'take this thing out' …"

"Yeah, so?"

"That *thing*," she intoned grimly, "only had six legs. Adult ticks have eight legs."

She paused, waiting for Donovan to respond. He didn't.

"That means what we saw was a larva…a baby. And ticks don't have just one baby."

"Oh, Jesus," Donovan grunted. "How many are we talking about?"

"I don't know. Maybe *thousands* of larvae, either new-born or about to hatch."

The sheer scope of the crisis his town was facing stunned Donovan speechless. But Dr. Sokolová was not done.

"And Chief," she continued, as if what she'd already said wasn't enough, "they're going to be hungry."

Chapter 30

MAYOR CANKERBY BEAMED WITH PRIDE as he strolled through the thick late-afternoon crowd on Main Street. This year's Harvest Moon Jubilee was off to a rollicking good start, with mild weather, good vibes, and every indication that it would be their largest attendance ever.

Main Street was roped off and closed to vehicles to accommodate the heavy foot traffic, and the sidewalks were busy with autumn-themed pop-up booths selling deep fried cheese curds, hamburgers and brats, homemade baked goods, and crafts and souvenir trinkets. As the mayor looked around, it seemed as though every other person he saw was sipping at hot apple cider or—for those in the crowd who wanted to start the party early—an official Harvest Moon Jubilee Bloody Mary, stacked high with pickle spears, olives, and sausage bites.

For the kids, the town had rented a small carousel, which was planted dead-center in the street. And every third or fourth business had some sort of game or other activity set up outside their doors to cater to the kiddos. Face and pumpkin painting booths, free root beer float giveaways, carnival games, and more.

That evening there would be a variety of activities to keep the celebration going well into the night. A free outdoor movie. Pig racing, courtesy of a mobile troupe from Missouri that was wrapping up its summer tour. And round one of the Miss Harvest Moon pageant, with the final competition slated for Saturday night. There was even a wet t-shirt contest at a small bar two blocks off Main Street, though it wasn't an officially sanctioned event of the Jubilee.

The mayor leaned forward slightly as he raised a heavily loaded bratwurst to his mouth. His first bite sent a cascade of ketchup, mustard, and pickle relish dribbling to the ground. Luckily, his awkward posture allowed his Sunday-best white suit to escape the culinary mayhem unscathed.

"Mr. Mayor!" Shep Davison shouted from not far away.

Still negotiating his messy snack, the mayor struggled for a moment to offer a handshake, but soon just shrugged and gave up. "How are you, Shep?" he finally laughed. "Wonderful turnout, don't you think?"

The plumber patted Mayor Cankerby on the shoulder and laughed back, "I think that's the first time you've ever *not* shook my hand, Mayor."

"It hurts me more than it hurts you, believe me," the mayor grinned, gobbling another careful bite of his brat. Then, through a mouthful, he repeated, 'Wonderful turnout."

"Sure is," Shep agreed, but quickly turned back to his task at hand. "Hey now, I need to focus here! I'm trying to get my litter round up and fed. You haven't seen any of my little ones, have you?"

The mayor nodded as he gulped down the last bite of brat, pleased to be able to help. Help a voter, win a vote. That was his philosophy.

"I have. Little Angel," the mayor answered. "Saw her chasing a squirrel over that way." The mayor wagged a finger in the direction of a small courtyard between two downtown buildings.

Shep wrinkled his face.

"That sounds about right. Okay, Mayor. Thanks, and congratulations! Wonderful turnout!"

And off Shep went, leaving a grinning Mayor Cankerby to bask in affirmation of his success.

#   #   #

Not so far away, seven-year-old Angela Davison tiptoed towards the fluffy squirrel she had been chasing. Though she'd never actually caught one before, this little fella had been moving so slowly through the courtyard—scavenging for fallen popcorn and other yummy morsels—that she thought she might have a chance this time. But even as she crept up on the munching rodent, a noisy clank snapped her attention away from the squirrel.

After her quick glance found nothing that could have caused the distraction, Angela turned back in the direction of the squirrel. But it was gone, perhaps startled by the same noise that had distracted Angela.

Slumping her shoulders, Angela had only a moment to pout before another startling clank drew her focus back in the other direction again. This time she zeroed in on what might have made the noise: the large, circular manhole cover just a few feet away from her in the road. But despite the noise, it appeared undisturbed.

Despite all the activity around her, Angela stayed focused on the manhole, waiting patiently for it to make its noise once again. It didn't take long. As she watched, the iron cover jolted suddenly upwards about four inches, landing back into place with another jarring clank.

Angela laughed out loud.

It reminded her of the time she put her cat in the hamper and then covered it with a sheet of cardboard. That cat must have jumped up to bang into the cardboard a half dozen times before finally knocking it out of the way and darting off into the other room. Standing there staring at the manhole cover, she wondered if there was a cat in there trying to get out.

Curious, Angela took a step towards it, and the heavy iron disc jumped again, this time further into the air. And when it clanked back down this time, it was no longer perfectly back in place. It came to rest awkwardly ajar.

Angela froze.

In the brief moment that the hole had been open, she saw clearly that it wasn't a cat banging its head against the heavy cover.

It was bigger.

Darker.

Uglier.

She shuddered. But frightened though she was, curiosity burned inside her. What was it?

Now only a yard from the manhole, Angela leaned forward, not willing to step any closer but desperately wanting a better look. Staring at the slight opening between the cover and the hole, she saw some movement and got ready for another big clank.

But when she yelped out in surprise, it wasn't because of what she saw. It was because of the hand on her shoulder.

"Angie Pants!" her father said as she jumped at his touch.

Angela craned around to look at him wide-eyed.

"Daddy!"

"There you are," Shep grinned. "Are you ready to get some dinner?"

Angela turned back to the manhole to see that the cover had not moved again.

"There's a monster in there," she exclaimed, pointing.

Shep laughed.

"Well, then we'd better get away from it," he grinned, turning Angela around and ushering her in another direction.

As they walked away, the manhole cover clanked one more time, flipping off from the hole and landing a foot away.

Chapter 31

"STOP!"

Kellerman's voice snapped with authority, bringing the entire hunting party to a halt once again.

They had just emerged from a heavily-wooded stretch into a large clearing when Kellerman—who had been marching silently along after handing the walkie-talkie back to Blonde—barked his command. Up ahead of them, deeper in the clearing, was the old hunters shack and elevated blind, but something else had triggered Kellerman's alert. Even as Emmaline and Jackson were just starting to recognize what it was, the three German mercenaries quickly unshouldered their Barrett M82 assault weapons and braced them against their shoulders.

"Vorwärts!" Kellerman barked. Blondie and Bug Eyes began to march toward the giant tick lying motionless in the dirt.

The closer they got to the creature—the two Germans' gun barrels aimed directly at the monster—the clearer it became that it was dead. With the creature facing away from them, they could see that the soft tissue of its rear flank had been ripped to shreds by multiple gun shots. Yellowish slime was splattered all over the creature and the ground around it. As they came up upon it, they could see additional brown and greenish gunk oozing from several of the wounds. Whatever internal organs occupied the mutant tick's body must have been ruptured by the gunfire, and whatever disgusting goop those organs contained was now leaking out to the ground.

"Bewachen Sie den Umkreis!" he commanded, and his two underlings swung their weapons in opposite directions. Each scanned and secured half of the surrounding woods.

Kellerman made a cautious approach toward the creature, his mouth agape. Nearing the beast, he let loose a curt laugh of sheer wonder, as if he had never before seen something so thrilling.

A few steps away, Emmaline was equally stunned. Though she'd already accepted the veracity of Jackson's story and the likely existence of the mutant creatures, seeing one of them up close and in the flesh was almost too much for her to comprehend. Unlike Kellerman's giddy excitement, however, its existence mortified Emmaline.

Lying flat on its belly, legs splayed in all directions, the monster still came up to her waist. She held her breath as she moved around it slowly, part of her convinced it was going to spring up with new life and lunge at her. But she was morbidly curious to see its face, and so she continued on until she was looking down at its head and mouthparts close up.

Two oval indentations at the top of its head must have been the eyes, she thought, though they were so flat and empty that she couldn't be sure if that's what they really were. Its curved palps hung askew, revealing the jagged barbs of its long chelicerae, as well as the speared end of its hypostome.

Emmaline couldn't suppress a shudder.

Stone dead, the creature was terrifying. She couldn't imagine a live one charging at her as it had at Jackson, who suddenly broke the silence.

"That's not it," he said.

"What?"

"I shot out the eye of the thing that attacked me, remember?" he explained. "This isn't it."

Jackson and Emmaline looked at Kellerman, who stared back at them with a tight-lipped grin.

"There's more than one of these things?" Jackson demanded.

"Of course, Mr. Reed," Kellerman said. "We estimate perhaps a dozen adult male—" Kellerman paused to articulate his new favorite word, "—*aberrations* like this one, perhaps more, perhaps less, have been causing all the trouble. Centurions, if you will. And then, of course, there is the queen, who we believe has remained close to her nest."

"Nest?" Emmaline gasped. "Ticks don't have *nests*. They don't have *queens*!"

"I see you've done some research," Kellerman mocked. "Bravo. But I assure you, Miss Blackdeer, that these ticks are unlike any that have ever been observed before. Both in stature and in behavior. These ticks have evolved."

Jackson's mind was still reeling from the earlier revelation.

"Wait. A nest implies that there are—"

"Eggs, yes," Kellerman confirmed. "And you are right to be concerned, Mr. Reed. Those hatchlings will—no doubt—be ravenous with hunger and eager to find the most readily available supply of food. And where do you suppose they would find such a bounty?"

Jackson and Emmaline both caught their breath in their throats, once again understanding the implications of what Kellerman was saying.

"The Jubilee," Emmaline uttered.

"Yes," Kellerman replied coolly, "but my employer has sadly determined that the scenario has now escalated beyond our control. And that means that I do not have time to sit back and enjoy watching these glorious titans transform your little hamlet into—what do you Americans call it?—an *all-you-can-eat buffet*! So, while my colleagues work to contain the situation in town, we need to complete things here. Now, if you will…"

Kellerman twitched the barrel of his Barret in the direction of the shack.

Even as Emmaline and Jackson considered everything that they had just heard, they turned and began to move as ordered. The grim reality of the circumstance—not just theirs, but all their friends and neighbors and colleagues in Tomahawk Hollow—overwhelmed them.

Then Jackson realized what Kellerman was saying.

"You're gonna kill the whole town," he declared in disbelief. "That's what you mean by 'contain'. You're going to wipe out everyone and everything."

Kellerman stood silent behind his dark glasses.

"How?" Jackson pressed, his anger escalating. "A bomb of some sort?

Something that can destroy the whole town?"

"What does that mean?" Emmaline asked. "What kind of bomb can destroy the whole town. It would have to be a—" She cut herself off, unsure she was right but unwilling to articulate the horrible thought.

"A nuclear bomb," Jackson finished her sentence. "You're going to set off a nuclear bomb to destroy the evidence, aren't you? And with it, the entire town and everyone in it."

Kellerman grinned.

"Not all the evidence," Kellerman noted, still confirming the journalists' worst fears. "The twenty-kiloton explosion my colleague will be triggering shortly will certainly obliterate the entirety of your small town, including the pesticide plant."

"That's the nest, isn't it?" Emmaline blurted out. "That why you have it all locked down. The plant is the nest."

Kellerman didn't respond, but his thin-lipped smirk was all the confirmation Emmaline needed.

"The blast will not, however, reach these woods," Kellerman explained, "so you and the remaining refuse inside this cabin will have to be incinerated separately." He paused. "And then that will leave just one more loose end, which my European colleagues will presently be arriving at the Institute of Parasitology to tie up."

Emmaline reacted to that, pleasing Kellerman.

"This is insane!" Jackson snapped. "You're going to cover up a mutant tick outbreak with an atomic explosion? How in Christ's name is that going to generate less scrutiny for your employer, whoever that is?"

"Blutmond Holdings," Emmaline revealed. "That's who's behind all this."

Kellerman chuckled humorlessly. "Very good, Miss Blackdeer. It's just a shame that you will never be able to share that information with your readers."

Then he turned back to Jackson. "And to address your concern, Mr. Reed, I assure you that a nuclear explosion in America's heartland is an event that any number of international terrorist organizations will gladly claim credit for. And I would imagine that a German-based chemical manufacturer will be quite low on the list of suspects, in any case. An invasion of chemically altered mutant arachnids, however, would quickly move my employer to the top of that list."

"Now, please," Kellerman concluded, "get inside the cabin."

Jackson and Emmaline looked at each other, both realizing that they had no choice or means of escape. And yet both refused to move.

Kellerman had had enough, raising his gun and pointing it at Emmaline. "I SAID INSIDE THE—"

A thunderous clap of gunfire from their flank dramatically cut off Kellerman's command.

They all turned to see Blondie crouched on one knee, his back to them, blasting shot after shot from his Barret into a phalanx of three giant ticks charging out of the trees.

"Zécken!" he cried in warning as the heavy .50 caliber rounds exploded from his weapon. His first shot missed entirely. But the second slammed into the scutum of the lead tick, splintering the protective shield and spraying a thick mist of yellow goo into the air. His third shot dislodged a huge chunk of its scutum, and the fourth slammed directly into its mouthparts, mangling its palps and sending the twitching beast crashing into the dirt.

Before any of them could react, another explosion spun them around. On the other side of the clearing, Bug Eyes had begun to open fire on a separate line of three more ticks racing in their direction.

Closer to the advancing ticks than his partner was, the very first blast from Bug Eyes' powerful cannon of a gun completely shattered the scutum of one of the ticks and destroyed its insides. The monster instantly dropped dead in its tracks.

It took Bug Eyes two shots to fell the second creature. The first blast just glanced the scutum, but the second slammed full-on into the monster's head. It exploded in a geyser of puss and arachnid viscera, leaving the thing dead before it hit the ground.

But even though Bug Eyes shuffled backwards defensively, the other mutant was on him before he could shoot again. A clawed front leg caught the long barrel of the Barret with enough force to swat it out of Bug Eyes' hands and send it flying. At practically the same moment, another knife-edged claw slashed towards his midsection. Bug Eyes tried to evade, but the razor sliced open his abdomen. His intestines unspooled to the ground amid a shower of blood as Bug Eyes gurgled and fell to his knees. The tick descended on him, its lethal claws casually shredding his weak flesh in a flurry of slashes and rips.

Kellerman raised and leveled his Barrett. Though he had the feeding mutant dead to rights, he froze, watching with giddy awe as the savage beast slaughtered his henchman. Blood and guts sprayed in every direction, bringing Kellerman to a state of near orgasmic wonder. He had never seen anything so elegantly barbarous in all his life, and he simply couldn't look away. And he certainly couldn't shoot and put an end to it.

Behind him, Blondie was in trouble.

With six rounds left in a ten-round magazine, he coolly shifted his sights, ready to take out a second of the two creatures on his side of the clearing. But when he pulled the trigger, his Barrett jammed, clicking impotently as the mutant tick rushed forward.

His composure faltering, Blondie squeezed again, but again the precision weapon would not discharge. The tick was about on him now. Fighting back full-on panic, he dropped the weapon and reached for the flamethrower dangling at his side. The tick overtook him, and though he managed to avoid the slashing claw meant to decapitate him, Blondie stumbled backwards. He fell to the ground, losing his grip on the weapon.

The marauding tick closed in on him, this time rocking briefly on its hind legs. As if prematurely celebrating its victory, the tick hovered there, ready to fall upon Blondie. But as it lowered its speared chelicerae for the kill, another rattle of gunfire sounded from above the fray, raining a salvo of bullets down on the tick.

Jackson and Emmaline—who to this point had been reduced to horrified spectators of the inconceivable battle—looked toward the sound of the shot. Above them, Elmer Dobbs leaned out the shooting window of the hunting blind. His KelTec PMR-30 in hand, Elmer blasted shot after shot in the direction of the tick about to kill Blondie. The first few shots simply snapped off chunks of its scutum. But when Elmer drew a line from the front of the monster to its back, the 9mm rounds began to riddle and tear open its more vulnerable rear flank. Twelve rounds into the barrage, the mutant's insides had been thoroughly scrambled. It collapsed down to the ground screeching and shuddering.

Alerted to the presence in the shooting blind, Kellerman swung around, elevated his weapon, and fired a booming shot. Stunned to see the man below aim his weapon in his direction, Elmer ducked out of the shooting window just in time. The thundering blast from the anti-material rifle tore a massive hole in the side of the elevated blind, effectively disintegrating the rotted wall and obliterating the entire upper portion of the enclosure.

Lowering his aim just slightly, Kellerman zeroed in on the lower half the blind. He was determined this time to destroy what was left of the small shelter and anyone who might be inside. But before Kellerman twitched his finger on the trigger, Jackson—who had just realized what he was doing—lunged at the German, barreling a shoulder into him just as the German squeezed off his shot. The impact altered his aim, and the .50 caliber round careened past the blind and smashed into the thick upper branch of a Northern Red Oak tree. The branch splintered into pieces, sending a shower of leaves and acorns cascading to the ground from the shuddering blow.

Infuriated, Kellerman regripped his Barrett and swung it like a blunt weapon. The attack caught Jackson across the jaw and sent him flailing backwards with a cry of pain. Then, reassessing the situation, Kellerman turned again to check on the status of the remaining tick on his side of the clearing.

Done with its bestial vivisection of Bug Eyes, the mutant tick had set its sights on Kellerman. It scampered forward, swinging a clawed front leg towards the German mercenary. But Kellerman reacted just in time to swat the organic razor away with the barrel of his gun.

Across the clearing, the bullet-riddled beast near Blondie had finally succumbed to its wounds and lay motionless in the dirt. Its companion hesitated, seemingly unsure whether to attack Blondie or to charge across the clearing toward Emmaline, who was trying to help Jackson to his feet. Blondie was closer, and in a flurry of flailing brown legs it raced around its fallen companion and charged at the fallen henchman.

With only a moment to react, Blondie rolled on his side and raised the nozzle of the flamethrower in defense. The mercenary's finger squeezed the trigger, and with a deafening roar a torrent of searing flames burst forth from the nozzle. The incendiary stream painted the tick with a furious red-orange cascade of heat and destruction. In the inferno's heart, the enraged tick—grotesque and relentless—writhed and twisted. Even as its carapace blistered and crackled, it flung its clawed legs wildly in all directions. A foul, acrid stench of flaming beast-flesh filled the air.

Discombobulated and wild with pain and fury, the mutant tick—now itself entirely ablaze and roasting from the outside in—raced off in a serpentine attempt to escape the conflagration. Behind it, Blondie clasped his hands over the bloody gash that had been torn out of his throat by one of the creature's flailing claws. Unable to vocalize his agony, he coughed sprays of crimson spittle over his own face in the few moments before death overcame him.

Blondie's killer, still aflame and lurching from side to side, nearly stampeded over Emmaline and Jackson. But the younger reporter shoved her mentor in one direction while diving herself in the other. The tick scurried right between them towards the cabin.

Oblivious now to what it was doing or where it was going, the tick just raced forward and crashed headlong through the door of the hunters shack, which—along with everything inside—had been drenched with gasoline and accelerant. Like a massive roman candle, an intense blast of searing heat and flames rose high above the trees and pummeled everything in its compass.

Emmaline and Jackson buried their faces in the dirt and grass to protect themselves from the blast. But the eruption knocked Kellerman, who remained engaged in virtual hand-to-hand combat with the last tick standing, violently off his feet. He went sprawling to the ground.

The explosion disoriented the tick. It scuttled uncertainly a few steps forward and then immediately a few steps backward. Despite its agitation, it recognized the sudden vulnerability of its enemy, and with instinctual clarity it rushed forward again to finish him off.

It took Kellerman only a moment to regain his wits. With the creature bearing down on him, he located his Barrett a few feet away in the dirt. He rolled towards it and reached out his left hand to grasp it, but the tick had reached him and planted one of its clawed feet down onto his arm. Only a reflexive twitch saved Kellerman's arm from being severed cleanly at the elbow. But he wasn't fast enough to avoid the clawed manus entirely. The razored appendage sliced easily through the German's upper arm, cleaving his bicep and fracturing the humerus.

Kellerman sat bolt upright and screamed. His left arm hung limply at his side by what remained of the shredded skin and tendons. Blood poured from the gaping wound, though the German tried to staunch the flow by gripping and squeezing it with his other hand. But with the tick ready to strike again, he kicked his feet wildly at the ground, trying to propel himself backwards and out of reach.

The creature pursued, knowing its kill was imminent. It closed ruthlessly on Kellerman.

But then it stopped.

Even with Kellerman well within its reach, the tick abandoned its pursuit when it spotted Jackson on the ground. Scuttling away from the retreating German, the tick turned towards Jackson and stared at him.

Stared at him with its one good eye.

As the thing squared off on him, Jackson saw its face and immediately recognized the mutant tick. And to his utter astonishment, he realized that the tick recognized him, as well.

Suddenly quaking with rage, the disfigured monster launched itself forward in a manic rush. Legs flailing in every direction, the tick unleashed a shrill wail as it charged wildly.

So stunned that he couldn't move, Jackson watched in horror as the monstrous beast attacked, closing the distance between them in just seconds.

The incensed mutant opened its palps to reveal its gnashing chelicerae. As it reached Jackson, it spread the barbed oral blades apart like scissors and lunged forward as if to snip him clean in half.

But salvation came with another crackle of gunfire from above.

Bracing himself against the remains of the blind and supported awkwardly by Dan, Elmer steadied his KelTech with both hands and squeezed off a barrage of shots at the attacking mutant. With each pull of the trigger, another round hammered into the body of the beast. The shots that hit scutum sent shards of organic armor flying. And the ones that hit the soft back of the monster ripped into flesh and produced leaping gushers of yellow puss.

Desperate to escape the relentless assault, the one-eyed tick scuttled recklessly backwards, unknowingly retreating directly into the raging inferno that once was the hunters shack. Before it even recognized the searing pain that it met there, the flames had engulfed it, and its juices boiled and burst from the blazing heat.

With the tick's grotesque shrieks rising from the flames, Kellerman wobbled to his feet. Despite his lame arm flopping hideously as he went, the German staggered on weakened legs towards the tree line.

Above him, Elmer aimed his weapon, tracking the ruthless mercenary who had tried to kill him as he ran. Drawing a final bead on his target, Elmer pulled the trigger.

But the KelTech just clicked.

The magazine was empty.

And Kellerman was gone.

Chapter 32

CHIEF DONOVAN'S SUV BOUNCED OVER The road as he raced back towards town. Evacuating Tomahawk Hollow in the middle of the Jubilee would be a herculean task. But he knew that he had to get townspeople and tourists alike out of there before the tick larvae hatched and figured out where to the find the nearest food supply.

And he doubted he could do it alone.

"Say again?" the gruff baritone voice groused through the SUV's speaker system.

Donovan was on the phone with Sheriff Calvin Buckley, who lived twenty miles away in the more populous Antigo. Buckley was on his fifth four-year term as the senior elected law enforcement officer in the county, and he had two ironclad rules for the deputies and cops in his jurisdiction. Number one, if a speeder is registered to vote in the county, a warning will do. Number two, never bother him during a Friday fish fry. And from the crowd noise behind him and the irritation in his voice, it sounded like Donovan was breaking rule number two.

But Donovan didn't care.

"Tomahawk Hollow is on the verge of a catastrophic mass casualty event!" he shouted over the combined roar of his own engine and the din of the northern Wisconsin supper club.

"Look, son," Sheriff Buckley grumbled, "I don't know what kind of bug you and that dime store Boss Hogg mayor of yours have up your bonnets…but I'm not going to scramble a bunch of my men on a Friday night just because you can't handle crowd control at your rinky-dink little festival down there!"

"Sheriff, I don't have time to explain it and you wouldn't believe me if I did," Donovan panted, "but I'm telling you the same thing I told the state police. I need every single badge and gun you've got down here right now! And I really don't give a shit if they don't have badges!"

At that moment, the screen on his dashboard flashed, signaling that he had another call coming in. According to the display, it was from "Jackson Reed."

"There's no call for that kind of language, son—" Sheriff Buckley started to object, but Donovan cut him off.

"Goddammit, Sheriff," Donovan barked, "get off your beer-battered fat ass and get me some reinforcements…or you're gonna be down about fifteen hundred votes by morning!"

Before the sheriff could respond, Donovan hung up and took Jackson's call.

"Jackson," Donovan answered quickly, "where are you?"

It was Emmaline on the line.

"Tim!" she shouted. "I know you don't believe us—"

"I've seen one, Em," Donovan interrupted. "And there's a lot more. I'm afraid they're going to find their way into town in the middle of Jubilee."

"Tim, listen," Emmaline struggled to raise her voice over the high-pitched scream of an engine and the howl of wind on her side of the line. "They will…but it's worse than that. There's a bomb!"

"What?"

"It's not just the ticks!" she shouted. "The mayor's goons have a nuclear bomb somewhere in town and they're going to set it off!"

Approaching downtown, Donovan was suddenly forced to reduce his speed. Something was wrong, as several festivalgoers appeared to be running in panic away from the town center. As he swerved to avoid one young couple running right down the center of the road, Donovan saw that the woman was supporting the man, who was limping badly. Both were hysterical, their faces and clothes painted with blood.

Oh my God, Donovan thought, *it's already started.*

"Did you hear me, Tim? They're going to cover this up by detonating a bomb to destroy everything!"

"Yeah, I heard you, Em!" Donovan shouted back, suddenly realizing how alone he really was. "I gotta go."

"Tim, wait!"

"What?"

"Tim," her voice was still loud but began to break, "I'm sorry."

"Em, this isn't a good—"

"No, listen!" she urged. "I know I screwed up, and I know I can never change what happened. But the last thing I ever wanted to do was hurt you, and…and I don't know what's going to happen. But it was the worst thing I've ever done…and I'm so, so sorry!"

Donovan's SUV went crashing through a sawhorse meant to stop traffic from entering the closed-down Main Street. As he entered the Jubilee grounds and slowed his vehicle down, Donovan could barely hear Emmaline anymore.

Through a dry mouth he muttered, "I gotta go, Em."

Slowing the vehicle to a full stop, Donovan's eyes were riveted to a scene more horrific than any he could have ever imagined.

The tick horde had overrun the Jubilee.

Chapter 33

EMMALINE HAD THE PHONE IN one hand and was hanging onto Jackson for dear life with the other as he gunned Elmer Dobbs' ATV over the Tomahawk Woods terrain. She knew the trails well, and even now at dusk she was able to direct Jackson to the quickest route out of the woods. When they emerged, they'd have a direct line across just two miles of undeveloped grassland to the abandoned pesticide plant.

Elmer and Dan had insisted on staying behind to avoid slowing them down. Restocked with weapons and supplies from the dead mercenaries, they were sure that the elevation of the blind would allow them to hold off any more tick attacks until help arrived. Having seen the terrible things in action twice now, they knew it was a priority for Emmaline and Jackson to destroy the nest.

"Please believe me, Tim! I'm sorry!" Emmaline cried, unsure if Donovan could hear her over the din or the racing ATV. "Tim?"

And then she looked at the phone screen and saw he'd already hung up on her.

"Dammit!" Emmaline swore, gripping Jackson more tightly after a severe bump nearly threw her from the vehicle.

Jackson shouted back over his shoulder, "Are you okay?"

"I lost him," she said.

"Just hang on," Jackson told her. "If we don't take care of that nest, it won't matter, anyway!"

Jackson turned the ATV up the main drive to the pesticides plant. Finally on solid ground after bouncing over two miles of field, he pushed the vehicle up to its top speed.

Approaching the front gate, Emmaline was silently coming to grips with the grim reality of the hazards they were about to confront. They were racing headlong into the monsters' lair and a waiting mob of hungry mutant hatchlings. On top of that, one or more of the German mercenaries was possibly inside waiting to ambush them. And at any moment, a nuclear bomb might detonate just a couple miles away and incinerate the town, the plant… and them along with it.

"Hold on!" Jackson's voice jolted her back to the moment as they barreled forward and slammed into the barrier. The chain securing the entry snapped, and the collision sent the metal gate clattering over the cement driveway. Nearly thrown free from the ATV by the jarring impact, Emmaline grabbed Jackson to steady herself and held on tight for the brief remainder of the drive to the plant's main entrance.

Having expected to encounter dozens of the grotesque creatures wriggling around the grounds, they were surprised to find the front courtyard deserted but for a single black van. Jackson slowed the ATV down as they approached it, unsure if any of the Germans were waiting inside.

Once they were close enough to see inside the van, they could tell that it was empty. The vehicle's rear hatch was open, and as they pulled around behind it, they saw a collection of weapons and equipment that had been rifled through and cast aside. Jackson stopped the ATV and they climbed off.

"Do you know how to use one of these?" Jackson asked Emmaline, retrieving one of the Heckler & Koch USP handguns laying in the van and handing it to her.

Emmaline took the weapon.

"Better than you do, I bet," she scoffed. Emmaline ejected the magazine, checked that it was full, and then snapped it back into place.

"Perks of growing up on a reservation?" he quipped, following her lead in checking the gun he grabbed for himself.

"Should we take anything else in here?" she asked, scanning around the van's cargo bay for anything else that looked helpful. There were some bigger guns, a cache of extra ammunition, communications equipment, and more.

"No, but help me with this, will you?" Jackson went back to the ATV to retrieve the flamethrower rig he had taken off Blondie. Emmaline didn't hear him, though, suddenly fixated on what looked like a crate in the back of the van. A tan tarp covered it.

"Emmaline?" Jackson nudged, coming up behind her as he strapped the twin tanks full of fuel and propellent to his back.

Carefully, Emmaline reached out and grabbed the tarp, pulling it away from the crate it concealed. In the dim glow of the van's ceiling lamp, they saw a square crate that measured about two and a half feet on all sides. A dozen holes the size of golf balls in each panel of the steel box allowed some visibility inside. However, it was too dark to make out any details of the large mass that occupied about half the crate.

"Give me your phone again," Emmaline said, taking the device from Jackson and igniting its flashlight. She trained the light onto the crate and looked closely again. This time she gasped at what she saw.

Jackson reacted verbally. "Jesus Christ."

The crate contained a large oval object about twice the size of a human head, which glistened with a sickly, translucent amber hue. The smooth surface of the gelatinous blob pulsed and shifted at erratic intervals, impelled by the twitchy, fluttering gyrations of the shadowy monstrosity inside it. They could not see the thing within clearly, but they both knew exactly what it was.

"Oh my God," Emmaline said. "They're taking an egg."

The two of them exchanged a somber glance, and then Jackson nudged her.

"Here, take this," he said, handing her the heavy backpack that Bug Eyes had been carrying through the woods. "Be careful."

Emmaline took it carefully. Not only because it was covered in blood—her mind flashed to the image of the mutant tick savagely ripping Bug Eyes to pieces—but also because Jackson had already told her what was inside.

The C4.

"Are you sure this is going to work?" Emmaline asked, failing to avoid getting the dead German's blood on her as she slipped her arms through the backpack straps.

"No," Jackson answered. "But if those tanks inside haven't leaked out, they should be filled with enough pesticides and other chemicals to blow this whole place sky high. Just so long as we can trigger it. Your source told you that they left it all there, right?"

Tightening the straps of the pack, Emmaline just shook her head. "It was just Miriam, Jackson. I don't know if I wanna bet my life on that."

"Well, that's what we're doing," he said, "so let's hope you're as good a reporter as I think you are."

Emmaline offered him a thin smile. Jackson put his hand on her shoulder for just a moment before giving her a nod.

"Okay, then," Jackson said. "Here we go."

The unlocked front entrance of the plant led them into a dark reception area that Jackson lit up with a small flashlight from the van. He swept the light over the floor looking for ticks. Finding none, he scanned the rest of the sparsely furnished entry room. A reception desk stood near the far wall, and near the front door were two chairs and a small table stacked with magazines several years out of date. Beyond the reception desk was a metal door marked "Authorized Staff Only," which Emmaline and Jackson made for.

Jackson tugged on it, but it was locked.

"Do you know where you're going?" Emmaline asked, unconsciously lowering her voice to a whisper.

"When they first came to town years ago, I toured the plant for a story," Jackson answered, matching her volume. "But I haven't been back since."

He pointed to a button behind the reception desk. "Hit that."

Emmaline reached over to press the button and the door buzzed. Gripping the knob in one hand and the flashlight in the other, Jackson pulled open the door to reveal a long, wide hallway on the other side.

Bathed in dull red light from caged emmergency bulbs mounted all along the walls, the hallway stretched a good fifty yards into the complex. A number of side halls appeared to branch off in various directions, and a half dozen doors concealed various offices and utility rooms. At the far end—if

Jackson recalled correctly—a set of heavy double doors would open into the main production area of the plant.

And the whole corridor was crawling with giant mutant ticks.

Chapter 34

DONOVAN JUMPED OUT OF HIS SUV and surveyed the bedlam unfolding all around him. What twenty minutes earlier had by an idyllic fall festival had been transformed into a sickening grotesquery. No matter where Donovan turned, ranks of the mutant brood swarmed horrified festivalgoers, savagely attacking anything and everything in their path. And over it all played a chaotic soundtrack of terrified screams, agonized cries, and the occasional pop of random gunfire.

Desperate to find a way to help but overwhelmed by the scale of the unfolding disaster, Donovan froze in place, able only to survey the state of pandemonium all around him.

The ticks seemed to be coming from all directions, but Donovan could see an open manhole forty feet away from him vomiting mutant ticks out onto the street. One by one they scrambled up from the sewer tunnel, identified potential victims, and joined the bloody fray. He took a halting step forward, thinking he could stanch the flow of predators from the sewer. But his attention was immediately redirected by the dozens of monstrous spectacles unfolding all around him.

On the sidewalk across from Donovan, an elderly man was pushing a card table full of baked goods over to shield himself from a frontal attack by two larvae ticks. But even as he backed away from them, another giant arachnid dropped down from a tree and knocked the old man to the ground.

Within seconds, his frail, flailing arms flopped down limply beside him as the small throng of blood-sucking fiends converged and tore away at his wrinkled flesh.

Further down the street, five of the freakish things surrounded a young woman who had somehow managed to get her hands on a long wooden shovel with a heavy metal blade. With both hands gripping the handle, she swung the makeshift weapon in a wide circle to keep her ravenous attackers at bay. One tick lunged forward, and the shovel blade smashed into its palps, eliciting a bestial screech and sending it rolling away. The impact compromised the woman's balance, though, and before she could reset herself the other ticks overran and quickly dissected her.

Closer to Donovan, a six-legged tick the size of a beanbag chair had mounted a screaming woman lying face down in the street. The length of one her legs was riven open, her calf shredded, and the monster was about to stab its hypostome into her back.

Finally propelled to action, Donovan detached his nightstick from his belt, and in one smooth motion lunged and swung the weapon at the monster. The blow struck with so much force that it tore the speared appendage right out of the larvae tick's mouth. A shower of yellowish goo spurt from the wound onto the injured woman's long hair as the furious creature shrieked and scrambled away.

Even as he turned the frantic woman over and helped her sit up, another six-legged demon was scampering towards them. Donovan let his nightstick clank to the asphalt street and unholstered his black Glock 19 handgun. He aimed low and fired three quick rounds from the semi-automatic pistol. With its larvae scutum still soft and immature, all three shots ripped into its body, tearing apart its glands and guts and dropping it dead at Donovan's feet.

From the corner of his eye, Donovan saw a young girl he recognized as Angela Davison standing in the middle of the street sobbing in abject terror. Not far away, two sinister creatures had spotted the vulnerable child and were scuttling towards her, one from in front and one from behind. Tears streamed down her cheeks as she helplessly watched the monster in front of her approach.

Donovan raced forward, closing quickly on the tick positioned between him and the young child. Though he knew he wouldn't be able to get a clean shot at the other one without endangering the girl, he had the closer one dead to rights. From ten feet away he began to fire—still running towards it—and all three 9mm rounds tore into the tick's idiosoma, killing it instantly.

The second tick had reached Angela, though, and Donovan—he realized helplessly—was too far away to do anything about it. Directly behind her now, the creature revealed its fearsome chelicerae, preparing to tear her apart.

But seemingly from nowhere, Shep Davison was suddenly there. He raced forward, plucked up his young daughter, and pulled her out of the path of the attacking creature. As Shep stumbled away with Angela in his arms, the young tick awkwardly swung one of its bladed feet towards them. Shep avoided the blow and raced away.

With nothing obstructing him now, Donovan raised his Glock and fired. The decisive blast slammed into the monster's face, which at near point-blank range exploded in a grisly splatter of tick goo.

Turning again to assess, Donovan was shocked to see the woman he had just saved laying on her back. A larvae tick had mounted her, its hypostome plunged into her cracked-open chest. The tick's body pulsed obscenely as it fed on the twitching woman, who watched it above her with horrified eyes for the few seconds before she died.

Donovan deflated.

This tick horde was like some medieval creature. Each time he managed to lop off one of its heads, two more would immediately spring up in its place.

Completely alone, Donovan realized that battling these things one by one would surely be a losing proposition. The likelihood of the sheriff or anyone else coming to his aid seemed remote, at best. And even if they did, he suddenly remembered, there was an even more cataclysmic danger facing Tomahawk Hollow.

A bomb.

And Donovan had a pretty good idea where it was.

Chapter 35

JACKSON AND EMMALINE BOTH GASPED at the horrors stretching out before them in the long corridor leading through the heart of Tomahawk Hollow Pesticides.

Though not as large as the ones they had encountered in the woods, dozens of the loathsome tick larvae clamored about on the concrete floor. Glistening with a slimy sheen of birth goo, the barely developed claws of the recent hatchlings *click-clacked* noisily on the hard surface as they scampered about.

Emmaline shuddered. Between the red glow of the floodlights, the teeming mass of savage demons, and the ghastly promise of what awaited them deeper inside the complex, it seemed to her that they were entering a passageway to hell.

"Stand behind me," Jackson said, snapping Emmaline out of it.

Aiming the flamethrower low, Jackson unleashed a furious stream of orange and yellow blaze at the creatures. Some managed to scamper away from the searing attack, lurching to one side of the hall or the other or retreating backwards to escape the assault. The ones that weren't quick enough got engulfed by the flames, writhing in torment.

One creature's exoskeleton crackled and sizzled under the blaze, oozing boiling secretions as the fire consumed it. Within moments, the monstrous thing succumbed to the intense heat and shriveled to a charred, lifeless husk reeking of scorched chitin.

Soon, the hallway was cleared, the mutant ticks either perishing under Jackson's assault or instinctively retreating in shrieking terror to the safety of the plant.

Jackson extinguished the flamethrower, and he and Emmaline looked at each other in surprise. Maybe they really could do this.

Advancing down the hall, they moved cautiously forward, careful to avoid the handful of ticks that were still in the final throes of their fiery extermination.

Along the way they passed closed doors that appeared to lead to a suite of offices, a utility closet, and a cafeteria. Just before reaching the double doors to the plant, they came to an extra-wide elevator. Neither would have thought anything of it, but the control panel on the wall featured what appeared to be a retina scanner. Again, they exchanged glances.

"Pretty serious security for a pesticides plant," Emmaline observed before they pressed on toward the end of the hallway.

When they reached the open double doors, a small cluster of tick larvae were gathered just inside the production area, blocking the entryway. Though just steps from Emmaline and Jackson, the six-legged monsters were too preoccupied to bother with the two interlopers. Jackson leveled the flamethrower, and the weapon belched a quick burst of searing flame towards the creatures. Just enough to make them scatter.

When Emmaline and Jackson saw what the ticks had been swarming over, they froze in their tracks.

It was one of the German henchmen. Or more precisely, *half* of one of the German henchmen. The upper half, cleaved off just above the waist. He was face down in a puddle of his own blood, arms splayed awkwardly and his shredded intestines spilling out the open base of his torso. What they could see of his flesh had been hacked and sliced and torn to pieces.

And his lower half was nowhere to be seen.

Even as they registered shock over the grisly remains, the nightmarish scene just beyond the mangled corpse demanded their attention.

The cavernous chamber still bore some resemblance to the pesticide production plant that it once was. Abandoned reactors and pumps and filtration systems were positioned throughout the plant just as they were on the day it closed its doors. And much deeper into the expansive industrial space, they could see a massive tank farm. In it, huge chemical storage cylinders sprouted from the concrete floor and rose forty feet high into a catwalk maze just under the vaulted ceiling.

But even though they could recognize what it once was, there was no denying what the gigantic apartment had become.

A nest of giant mutant ticks.

Eggs—some the size of soccer balls and others big as watermelons—were strewn and piled everywhere across the expanse of the plant. The tawny, veined pods pulsated with menace, the twitching mutants inside impatiently awaiting their hellish birth.

And there were thousands of them.

All around them, wobbling on unsteady legs, newly hatched tick larvae clambered over and around the mounds of gelatinous eggs. As Jackson and Emmaline watched, five of these smaller creatures converged on one of the throbbing pods. Inside it, one of their brethren was struggling to escape.

At first, the fetal monster merely pushed and punched against the gummy confines of the egg. But when one of its underdeveloped claws finally punctured the surface and poked out into the open air, the action triggered the other ticks into a frenzy. The little demons slashed and tore at the outer casing of the egg like five mutant midwives, eagerly hastening the birth of another savage predator to join their crusade of mayhem and slaughter. When the slime-covered hatchling finally stepped free of its mangled sanctum, the others began to pick away at the viscid globs of egg viscera that still clung to it.

Thoroughly disgusted by the profane spectacle, Jackson aimed the flamethrower and unleashed a torrent of fire into their midst. The blaze engulfed the six larvae, flaming gel adhering to their bodies and igniting each of them into scampering, screaming balls of fire. None got far before they succumbed, shriveled, and died.

"I'll kill these things one by one if I have to," Jackson vowed, stepping forward towards another pile of mutant eggs.

Emmaline grabbed his arm and held him back.

"Wait," she said, motioning to the revolting remains of the German goon. "Those things couldn't have done *that*."

He looked up at her grimly, realizing she was right.

"There's something bigger in here," she warned. "*Much* bigger."

As if on cue, a booming roar thundered from the depths of the plant. Unlike anything Jackson or Emmaline had ever heard before, the rumbling caw pounded their eardrums and filled them with dread. Icy fingers of fear reached into their chests and squeezed their hearts as an unseen colossus answered the dying cries of the slain larvae with a bestial declaration of violence and rage.

"I don't think we're going to have a lot of time," Jackson stood, struggling for a moment to get the words out. "We have to get that—" he pointed to the backpack full of explosives, "—over there." He gestured towards the tank farm at the far end of the chamber.

Without waiting for a reply, Jackson moved forward, discharging another belch of fire in front of him to startle a pack of scampering tick larvae out of his path.

"Make sure they don't close in behind us," Jackson directed, but Emmaline had no idea how she could prevent it.

They had only gone a few steps forward when another thunderous din rose from the direction of the tank farm, inciting the tick hatchlings into convulsions of excitement. This time there was no need for Jackson and Emmaline to imagine what kind of ungodly creature could have made the sound. This time the monster tramped out of the concealment of the tank farm and into plain view.

Jackson and Emmaline stopped dumbfounded in their tracks.

Standing nearly fifteen feet tall, the monster tick had the massive body of a bull elephant. With eight thick brown legs splayed all around it, the thing had a wingspan approaching thirty feet. Its head and mouthparts alone were the size of a kitchen cabinet, its chelicerae extending forward like industrial chainsaws wrapped in thick barbed wire. As it rumbled past the chemical tanks and through the nest, its immense legs sent clusters of turgid, slimy eggs skidding in all directions.

Chapter 36

MAYOR CANKERBY WAS AGHAST.

Horror had descended on Tomahawk Hollow like a summer storm. One minute, friends and families were enjoying a delightful autumn festival full of laughter and cheer. The next, they were all thrust into the midst of an unimaginable nightmare. It happened so fast that he barely had the wits about him to seek shelter.

But after watching Del Evans unsuccessfully try to fight off two of the attacking ticks, Cankerby knew enough to get indoors.

Without a weapon to defend himself, the Main Street butcher had screamed in pain when one of the ticks sliced a razor claw into his thigh. When he fell weakly to his knees, the same beast finished the job by stabbing its spiked hypostome straight into his face. The two spikes sunk into Del's eye sockets, mashing his eyeballs with a stomach-turning squish. And when the two ticks began to slice and slash him to pieces, Cankerby morbidly thought that if Del could have witnessed the assault from a distance, the veteran butcher might have felt some professional appreciation for their work.

But the mayor did not.

On his chubby, trembling legs, Mayor Cankerby bumbled down Main Street. In his mad dash for City Hall, he had to swerve several times to avoid stumbling over friends and constituents who were being eaten alive by the mutant swarm. And it was only when he'd nearly reached his refuge that he realized that he was being pursued himself.

Looking back over his shoulder, the mayor was horrified to see a frenzy of long brown legs flailing about as three of the scampering brutes raced after him. Cankerby cried out and stumbled, practically falling to the sidewalk and allowing the ticks to overtake him. But he caught himself and reached the door to City Hall. Flinging it open, he slipped inside and yanked it closed just in time.

One of the ticks banged headlong into the glass door, bouncing almost comically off it. As the mayor fumbled to lock the door, its two companions began to scrape and claw at the glass in a futile attempt to reach the substantial meal that was now just out of their reach. They were too small and weak to fracture the clear barrier, though, and soon all three scuttled off in pursuit of easier prey.

The mayor exhaled for what seemed like the first time since the attack on the Jubilee began. Covering his face with his hands, he imagined for a moment that he could make the whole nightmare go away simply by blocking it from his sight. But a sudden banging on the door startled him out of that fantasy.

On the other side of the entrance, Colleen Lupinski was slapping one hand against the glass to get his attention while tugging futilely at the door handle with the other one. She and her husband Doug had been among the first to report signs of trouble at their farm, but they'd agreed to be discreet about it so as not to cause any problems for the Jubilee.

"Mayor!" she cried. "Open the door! Let me in!"

With two long lacerations carved across her face and a blouse soaked red with blood, Colleen looked like she'd already survived an initial attack. Now in near hysterics and with barely enough strength to pound on the door, it was clear that she couldn't survive another.

But the mayor didn't move.

"Help me, please," she pleaded, tears mixing with blood and streaming down her cheeks. "They got Doug! Please, God, please help me!"

With the smallest of gestures, Mayor Cankerby shook his head.

There wasn't a chance in hell that he was opening that door for her or anybody else.

Colleen opened her mouth to unleash a scream, but instead she retched a thick spray of blood that splashed onto the window just in front of Cankerby's face. Her eyes bulged wide with shock as the rest of her body froze. When she collapsed forward against the door and tumbled to the ground, the mayor could see the tick that had leapt onto her back and speared her from behind.

The mayor turned away, lightheaded and gagging.

He wobbled momentarily on unsteady legs, fighting to suppress the roiling mash of half-digested bratwurst and fried cheese that threatened to spew up from his stomach. But it all came erupting out when he saw the remains of Miriam Todd on the floor.

Stumbling backwards away from the desiccated corpse—split open at the middle and drained of blood—the mayor wiped what was left of his dinner off his mouth and chin. His assistant's glossy dead eyes seemed to stare right into his, and her mouth was frozen open in a silent howl of agony. Cankerby felt around behind him for the door to his office, pushed it open, and backed in, slamming it shut behind him.

In near blackness, the mayor fumbled with the lock, snapping it in place to secure the room. Then he felt his way to his desk in the dark and collapsed into his chair. From just beyond the window looking out into the courtyard behind City Hall, the mayor could hear a child screaming. Even as his eyes adjusted to the faint light, he refused to turn around and look. There was nothing outside that he wanted to see.

Now just able to make out the objects around him, Cankerby reached for the phone on his desk.

The National Guard, he thought. *I'll call the Governor and have her scramble the National Guard!*

He started to dial the number he knew by heart but stopped abruptly.

What will I tell them? he thought, sweat beading on his forehead. *Too many people know I tried to cover this up. What if Kellerman hasn't taken care of them all?*

And where the hell is Kellerman, anyway? he continued to ponder angrily. *He was supposed to eliminate these things! He was supposed to take care of all of this!*

The mayor slammed the phone back onto the cradle.

And then he stopped and listened for a moment, sickened by what he *didn't* hear.

The child's screaming had stopped.

Maybe she ran off, he thought, though he didn't really believe it. *Maybe someone rescued her.*

But Mayor Cankerby knew that was a lie.

In his mind's eye he saw Colleen Lupinski vomit blood and collapse into the door like a rag doll. He saw Miriam Todd lying violated and drained on the cold floor of City Hall. He saw longtime friends and strangers alike slaughtered by unthinkable monsters, screaming as they met their horrific end. And then he imagined the terrible fate of that young child in the courtyard. Was it one of Shep Davison's kids? Or maybe little Emily Dickerson, whose parents were among his most enthusiastic supporters? *Or maybe,* he thought—he hoped, actually—*it was some tourist's child.* That would sting just a little less, he decided.

Then, with his hands cupped over his mouth and his mind racing to imagine some acceptable outcome to all this, he heard it for the first time.

Click.

The mayor caught his breath, unsure if he'd imagined it or actually heard it. He listened closely for a moment and then —hearing nothing— exhaled sharply in relief.

Until it came again.

Click click click.

Even in the dim light the mayor could see one spindly brown leg reach up from the other side of his desk and plant itself on its surface— *click*—followed by another. *Click*! Then the monster's face appeared, palps twitching angrily. And then the rest of it, as it crawled deftly up onto the desk, *click click cllcking* on the wood.

He'd locked himself in with the unholy beast!

Staring with horror into the mutant tick's flat, dead eyes, the mayor's muscles tightened and locked. He could feel the frantic trembling of his hands but couldn't will them to move. Instead, he sat there, frozen in place, immobilized by soul-crushing dread while the creature moved towards him.

Click click click.

For a moment, the tick hesitated, its monstrous face just inches from the mayor's.

In his mind, Cankerby screamed in terror, but no sound escaped his mouth, which simply twisted open in a miserable parody of his crocodile smile.

Then he felt warmth soak his trousers as his bladder released.

And then a crippling pain—more intense than anything he had ever experienced—exploded through his left arm.

Had it come a few seconds earlier, the heart attack might have spared him from a grislier end. But at that exact same moment the hungry tick struck, plunging its hypostome straight into the mayor's half-open mouth. Its speared end tore Cankerby's tongue clean off before punching savagely through the back of his neck. Then, in one final slash and snip of its jagged chelicerae, the tick sheared the mayor's head clean off.

And that was officially the end of Mayor Silas Cankerby's political career.

Chapter 37

THE APPEARANCE OF THE QUEEN tick stunned Jackson and Emmaline.

Larger than any animal either had ever seen in real life, the monster looked like something out of a science fiction movie. A miracle of modern special effects that could only be achieved by teams of computer artists and programmers. But instead of towering over them at the multiplex in Rothschild or the Palace Twin Theatre in Antigo, this fantastic creature was lumbering towards them across the plant floor.

Without even thinking, Emmaline gripped her HK tightly, aimed high, and fired a shot at the beast. Though still a good distance away, the target was hard to miss, and the round hammered into the creature's body just past its head.

Jackson dropped the flamethrower, letting it dangle by its hose at his side, and raised his own HK. Joining Emmaline, he blasted a salvo of heavy caliber rounds at the enraged queen.

In a matter of seconds, they had combined to plug a dozen shots into the beast. But when they paused to evaluate their work, they saw that the onslaught had done nothing to slow its advance. Some bullets had bounced ineffectually off the queen's steel-like scutum, and even the shots that found unprotected patches of her body simply lodged into the thick, leathery surface of her exoskeleton.

Jackson gasped.

Not only was the giant monster unscathed by their fusillade of gunfire, but it had also positioned itself directly between them and the tank farm. He calculated quickly and made a snap decision.

"You go!" he bellowed at Emmaline. "Find another way to get to those tanks! I'll keep her busy!"

"What?" Emmaline was stunned.

But Jackson didn't answer. Regripping the flamethrower, he began to run towards the queen tick.

Emmaline watched, mouth hanging open, as Jackson rushed forward to confront the monster. She had no idea how she was going to get to the tanks with that monster in the way, much less how to detonate a backpack full of plastic explosives. Her mind racing, she darted her eyes around trying to find a pathway past the creature.

And then she saw it.

It wasn't a great option, but it was her only option.

Emmaline ran back toward the entrance of the production area. She stuffed the HK handgun into the waist of her jeans and grabbed a lower rung of the wall-mounted ladder next to the double doors. Hoisting herself up just as a band of hungry tick larvae converged around her, she scrambled up the first few rungs until her feet were clear of their little slashing claws. Then, taking a deep breath, she started to climb up to the catwalk above.

On the floor of the plant, the unlikely battle between Jackson and the queen tick was escalating quickly.

The moment that Jackson had begun to charge at the eight-legged gargantuan, the queen tick seemed to take up his challenge, speeding her own rush forward and letting loose a feral wail.

When the mismatched combatants had closed to within fifty feet of each other, Jackson skidded to a stop. Raising the flamethrower and bracing himself, he unleashed the full fury of the incendiary weapon towards the monster. The raging column of fire blasted into the giant's face, enveloping its twitching mouthparts and eyes and washing over its front legs and underbelly.

The blistering pain from the blast shocked the queen. In her awkward attempt to make a sudden stop, she stumbled forward on her front legs and crashed headfirst into the concrete floor.

Jackson didn't relent, maintaining the flaming onslaught as he pressed on closer and closer to the raging behemoth.

Her insides boiling from the unyielding assault, the queen tick scrambled back to her feet, screeching and lurching from the unfamiliar sensations of pain and fear. She shuffled backward, turned clumsily, and then lumbered away back towards the tank farm.

Jackson painted her hind quarter with his molten spray, but the creature's long legs carried her faster than Jackson could run. Once she was out of range, he extinguished the flames and watched her—puddles of fire still clinging to her scorched carapace—disappear behind the forest of massive tanks.

Jackson grinned.

He had her on the run.

The rain of fire had sent the smaller ticks retreating to the far reaches of the plant. However, the profusion of gluey eggs littered and piled everywhere around him slowed Jackson as he moved toward the tank farm. Fighting the urge to blast away with the flamethrower—he realized that he needed to preserve its fuel for the queen—Jackson slogged and kicked his way through the egg swamp.

As he went further, the piles of glutinous pods grew bigger and bigger, until some mounds were so immense that they stood higher than Jackson's head and forced him to circle around them.

All the while, he watched the queen tick just beyond the tanks. In the murky red glow bathing the chamber, Jackson could see her appear one moment and disappear the next. As she stalked around from behind one giant cistern to another, Jackson wondered if he was hunting her or she was hunting him.

It didn't matter, he knew. He had reached the tank farm, and one way or another they would be face-to-face again soon.

Or maybe not.

Jackson heard the crackle of gunfire before he felt the searing pain explode like a firecracker in his upper leg. The leg gave out and he crumbled to the floor. From across the plant, the *rat-a-tat-tat* report of an automatic weapon sent a flurry of bullets sailing over him and into the towering dune of pods just beyond.

Leg burning and eyes stinging, Jackson rolled over to see what had happened.

Kellerman strode towards him, grinning maniacally.

Chapter 38

WHEN DONOVAN BURST INTO THE lobby of the Main Street Inn, the carnage that greeted him was not so different than that on the street outside.

At various locations in the lobby, three young ticks were mounted atop their bloody and broken victims, their repugnant feeding ritual well underway. Around them, a frantic melee played out as more mutant monsters attempted to claim their meals.

Fighting the instinct to stop and help, Donovan darted through the lobby and sprinted up the main staircase, taking the steps three at a time. Something told him that he didn't have a moment to spare.

Reaching the second floor, he paused, looking from side to side until he recognized the direction he needed to go.

Halfway down the hallway, one of the creatures was in his path. It was bigger than the others he'd seen on the street, with more mass and eight long legs instead of six. An adult, Donovan reckoned, wondering if his gun would be as effective against the larger tick.

Only one way to find out.

Donovan raised his Glock and squeezed the trigger, but the gun didn't fire.

Empty.

Dropping the weapon, Donovan raced towards the tick. It crouched low on its eight legs, as if getting set to launch itself at the oncoming human.

But just as he got close enough for it to slash two clawed front legs at him, Donovan leapt into the air, vaulting over the enraged beast before it could strike. In a fury, the thing waved its claws at the air and scuttled about. But Donovan was well beyond its grasp.

The door to Room 217 was slightly ajar, so Donovan hammered his shoulder into it and smacked it open.

When he burst into the room, the first thing he saw were two dead tick larvae lying on the floor, yellow puss spattered around a plentitude of bullet wounds. Just beyond them, one of Kellerman's henchmen had a metal suitcase open on the bed. His HK USP handgun rested next to it.

Donovan immediately recognized the metal case as the suitcase bomb he was after.

The German mercenary reached for the gun and spun towards the door. But bounding across the small room, Donovan pummeled him before he could get off a shot. The two men bounced over the bed and rolled off the other side, crashing hard as the HK USP went skidding away across the floor.

Donovan landed hard on top of the German, momentarily stunning the soldier-for-hire. But before Donovan could get control of him, the more experienced fighter thrust upwards. The forceful shove flung Donovan away, sending him careening into one of the legs of an ornate wooden desk by the window. The long, beveled leg broke off on impact, and the whole heavy stand came clattering down on top of Donovan's shoulders and back.

Though disoriented, Donovan reached for the snapped-off desk leg. Pushing himself up to his feet, he swung the broken, jagged end of the improvised weapon out in front of him. The German was too quick for him, though, slapping the desk leg out of his hand and arcing a compact right hook into Donovan's jaw. The powerful blow stunned the chief and knocked him a step backwards. When the mercenary closed quickly and repeated the action, it battered Donovan into the wall behind him and sent him sliding to the floor.

The German turned back towards the suitcase bomb, determined to complete his task. But despite the pain and weakness that might otherwise have stopped him, Donovan lunged desperately across the floor and wrapped his arms around his adversary's ankles. Legs tangled, the mercenary cursed and toppled back to the floor.

Try as he might, Donovan couldn't keep hold of the German's kicking legs. A booted foot caught him on the top of his head, again stunning him long enough for his enemy to break free.

In a flash, Kellerman's henchman was back on his feet and at the bomb. On a mission, he rapidly clicked buttons and flipped switches into place while Donovan scrambled around on the floor.

It took only a few moments for the German to complete his task. When the proper sequence had been registered, a handle grip with a trigger on it snapped up from the contraption.

Gripping the handle and resting his finger on the trigger, the German craned his head around to locate his foe.

Donovan was on his feet. In his hand he held the HK pistol aimed directly at the soldier-for-hire's face.

The German goon sneered.

"You're too late," he taunted. "We all die now."

But then he screamed.

The screeching ejaculation of shock and agony startled Donovan. And when the howling mercenary brought his arm around, it was missing its hand. Geysers of blood spurted gruesomely from the German's severed wrist as he waved it wildly in front of him. But Donovan ended his macabre gyrations with a single, decisive shot to the head.

The mercenary was dead before he hit the floor.

As Donovan watched, the tick that he'd evaded in the hallway crawled up onto the bed, waving one of its blood-streaked front claws with menace. Next to it was the severed hand it had hacked off the German before he could squeeze the trigger.

Donovan exhaled and smiled wryly.

"Thanks for the help," he said, casually leveling the HK USP and firing.

Once again, the gun in his hand just clicked.

"Goddammit," Donovan swore. That was the second time an empty magazine had spared that tick a bullet to the face.

And then the monster lunged.

Donovan lurched out of the way to avoid the attack, spilling to the floor in the process. The creature landed just beyond him. As the tick scampered around to face him, Donovan reached for a lamp that had fallen from the broken desk. With a cry, he hurled it towards the beast. The projectile hit the tick squarely, but bounced weakly away, and the mutant scuttled at Donovan, baring its barbed chelicerae.

Still laying on the floor, Donovan grabbed for the small wooden chair that had sat by the desk. Grunting, he heaved it awkwardly at the monster. This time the impact jolted the tick back slightly, but again the angry creature gathered itself and advanced.

Out of time now, Donovan stretched for the last potential weapon still within his reach.

The busted desk leg.

Grasping the jagged, spiked end where it had broken, Donovan twisted on the floor and swung the blunt end around. The blow struck one of the tick's outstretched claws, knocking it out of the way just as it was slicing towards Donovan.

The monster quaked with rage and lunged again. From his back, Donovan managed another floundering swing of the club, this time crunching into the tick's barbed mouthparts.

The thing screeched and stumbled, but its savage ire would not be denied.

Crouching back and low on its hind legs, the monster coiled itself for one final attack. Donovan desperately reversed his grip on the makeshift spear and twisted it around just as the tick rose up to its full height, balanced on its two back legs, and then fell forward. When the mutant beast descended onto him, Donovan aimed the speared end of his improvised lance and braced. The jagged tip of the broken wood tore into the tick's soft underside, its weight impaling the shaft deep into its body until it was run clear through.

As warm yellow puss leaked down over Donovan's hands, he held the stake tight and wrenched it around to scramble the creature's insides. The thing shrieked and shuddered, slashing its claws toward Donovan, but it was unable to get at him pinned there under its body. By the time the frenzied convulsions slowed and then stopped, Donovan was covered in putrid ooze.

With a grunt, Donovan shoved the mutant carcass off himself. Nearly spent, he braced himself on the bed and pushed himself up. With a disgusted groan he wiped the tick goo off his hands on the bedspread.

Sitting on the bed, he swatted the severed hand away from the bomb and to the floor. After all he'd seen today, it wouldn't have stunned him to see the disembodied appendage reach up and trigger the nuke all on its own, so he wasn't taking any chances. Then he stared at the mechanism and tried to determine how to disable it.

As he studied the switches and knobs on the device, he heard something rise above the pandemonic chaos on the street.

Gunfire.

Not the random, single gunshots that he had heard going off helter-skelter when he arrived at the Jubilee grounds. Now it was sustained, organized gunfire from what sounded like multiple weapons.

Donovan got up and went to the window.

In just the limited area he could see from above, at least a dozen well-armed, uniformed officers were advancing down Main Street. Organized and deliberate, they marched in tight three-man formations, clearing the street and exterminating the mutant ticks one-by-one. It was hard for Donovan to see from where he was, but they appeared to be the State Police.

Donovan breathed a heavy sigh of relief.

After all these years, his backup had finally arrived.

Chapter 39

KARL KELLERMAN MOVED THROUGH THE hellscape of the pesticide plant like a raging demon.

One arm hung limply at his side, but he gripped a bulky Brügger & Thomet MP9_machine pistol in the other hand. His face was charred and cut in several places, and his shirt was wet and soaked through with blood. Marching across the plant, he looked as if he had crawled out of his own grave to visit revenge on those who had thwarted his mission in Tomahawk Hollow.

"Jackson!" Emmaline—startled by the gunfire and seeing Jackson collapsed and bleeding on the floor below—screamed from the catwalk.

Spotting her there above him, Kellerman spun around and unloaded a burst of gunfire in her direction. Emmaline ducked low to avoid the attack, and the barrage of slugs clanged and sparked off the tight-mesh steel floor of the catwalk. When she stood up again, she had her own weapon in hand and fired down at the German mercenary.

Vulnerable to attack from above, Kellerman turned and ran in the opposite direction. Emmaline pursued him with a steady line of gunfire. Each shot hammered into the concrete floor behind Kellerman or obliterated one of the jellied pods he ran through. After several shots, her gun was empty and the shooting ceased.

Kellerman stopped and looked back at Emmaline. Seeing that she was out of ammunition, he raised his machine pistol and fired off another angry fusillade. But he was too far away to make it count.

Looking quickly around, Kellerman scanned the expanse of catwalk above. He spotted the wall-mounted ladder and reached for it. With only one good hand to work with, he discarded the MP9, grabbed the highest rung he could reach, and heaved upwards. He felt for a footing, braced himself, and then—quick as a wink—let go of the rung with his hand and snapped it up to the next one. Thus began his arduous one-armed climb up the ladder.

Emmaline saw Kellerman and calculated it would take him at least a few minutes to reach her. Sprinting along the catwalk, she approached one of the massive pesticide storage tanks deep in the farm. She unslung the backpack and kneeled down to empty its contents onto the metal platform.

Thick blue tape bound a half-dozen blocks of C4 together. A tangle of coiled wires twisted into and around the blocks and ultimately to a small detonator attached to the explosives. The digital numbers on the timed device were dark, and Emmaline frantically examined the keypad to figure out how to use the device.

It looked like a small alarm clock or kitchen timer, and when Emmaline pressed a button with an I/O on it, the numbers lit up. The timer was preset for five minutes. That didn't seem like much time to escape to Emmaline. But not wanting to mess around with the device, she decided quickly that it would have to be good enough.

Emmaline measured out several long strands of extra blue tape from a roll at the bottom of the backpack, tearing them off with her teeth and hanging them off the railing of the catwalk. When she had enough to work with, she stood and went to work affixing the incendiary bomb to the tank. Hands shaking and heart thumping, Emmaline was convinced that at any second her damp palms would lose their grip and send the device plummeting into the massive piles of eggs below.

Despite her fumbling, Emmaline quickly secured the bomb to the tank. Drawing a deep breath, she pressed "Start," and the digital clock began to count backwards from five minutes.

4:59

4:58

4:57

4:56

4:55

Emmaline shivered, her whole body vibrating with the realization of what she just sent in motion.

When she turned around, Kellerman was just forty feet away from her on the catwalk. Still panting from the awkward, grueling climb, he stomped towards her with a look of unhinged determination. From a sheath on his thigh, he extracted a knife with a long, serrated blade.

"I'm afraid I cannot allow you to detonate that bomb, Miss Blackdeer," Kellerman snarled as he approached.

"What are you talking about?" Emmaline called back. "You're going to set off a *nuke*!"

"If my man succeeds, yes, none of this will matter," Kellerman snorted. "But if he fails—and I pray that he fails—then these glorious creatures will drain every last drop of blood left in your inconsequential little hamlet.

"You see, Miss Blackdeer, my employer was wrong! If they could see what I've seen, they'd know that these—these *wonders*—must be allowed to survive!"

Kellerman had snapped.

Even with his guttural German accent, his voice pitched higher and faster than normal. His whole body practically trembled with a manic fervor as he ranted on.

"Don't you understand?" he huffed. "These are miracles of nature. Savage and relentless killers capable of initiating a radical reorganization of this planet's evolutionary hierarchy. We will not exterminate *them*, Miss Blackdeer. *They* will exterminate *us*!"

Every word had brought Kellerman a step closer to Emmaline. By the time he finished, he was on top of her.

With a growl, Kellerman jabbed the knife forward, forcing Emmaline to hop back to avoid the attack. The German pressed, slashing again. Already near the end of the platform, Emmaline ranged back as far as she could, and the blade just missed slicing into her stomach.

The momentum of Kellerman's mighty thrust left him momentarily off-balance and exposed, and Emmaline struck. Clenching her hands together into a double fist, she hammered directly into the gaping wound in Kellerman's arm. On impact, he wailed in agony, dropping down to one knee from the intense pain.

As he rose again, Emmaline gripped the rails of the narrow catwalk—one hand on each side—and thrust herself up. With as much force as she could muster, she kicked both feet violently into the German's chest. Stumbling back, Kellerman tripped over his own feet and tumbled hard onto the metal platform.

Emmaline checked the deteriorating clock behind her.

3:44

3:43

3:42

3:41

When she turned back around, Kellerman was back on his feet.

But rather than coming forward, he was standing awe-struck, his mouth hanging open. An unsteady hand rose to pull his sunglasses off, revealing bulging, colorless eyes nearly bereft of all pigment. The ghostly twin orbs widened, and Kellerman's chest rose and fell with deep, excited breaths as a depraved wonder seemed to overwhelm him.

Emmaline followed his eyes down to the floor of the plant, where the queen tick stalked out from behind the redwood forest of tanks.

"Lieber Gott," Kellerman murmured, seeing what he imagined to be the mother of humankind's eradication rumble into view. "It's magnificent!"

Below them, Jackson was still on the floor, now pulling his belt tight around his upper thigh where Kellerman's shot had shattered his femur. Had the bullet hit just six inches higher, it might have struck the fuel tank on his back and turned Jackson into a ball of fire. Regardless, the shot had done its job. By the time he secured the makeshift tourniquet into place, he had already lost enough blood to leave him lightheaded and weak.

And the pain was excruciating.

Even still, when he saw the queen tick come out from behind the tanks and spot him there on the floor, he knew he would somehow have to move. Despite the agonizing throb in his lower body, Jackson struggled up on one leg, an exhausting exercise that went for naught. Unable to stay upright, he teetered over and fell, crashing back down.

Not far away now, the monster tick was practically galloping on her eight legs, determined to eradicate this pest that had inflicted such pain on her and her brood.

As she approached, Jackson realized that even if he could get up again, escape on foot in his present condition would be impossible.

Instead, he looked around quickly, calculated, and began a desperate crawl towards a heaping dune of tawny pods just a few feet away.

With the queen tick closing in angrily, Jackson reached the base of the egg hillock and wildly began to burrow into it. Heaving massive pods away and pushing forward with his one good leg, Jackson shoveled and kicked and squirmed and fought his way into the gummy, slimy mass of gestating ticks. Despite the tiniest of air pockets around his head and the crushing weight pressing down on him, he forced himself to breathe. With small, quick breaths, he forced the mucid oxygen into his lungs as he sought refuge from the monster.

Just as Jackson's feet disappeared into the pile, the queen tick reached the mountain of eggs and stopped, uncertain. Then, unleashing an enraged roar, she swung a leg into the glutinous mass. With claws as big as snowblower blades, her furious stroke sent a dozen pods catapulting through the air and another dozen splattering across the floor. Raving, she slashed and stomped with her front claws, demolishing scores of eggs and slaughtering multitudes of her own progeny with each crazed blow.

Inside that fetid cocoon of ripening mutations, Jackson could perceive the fetal ticks stirring all around him. Sensing the proximity of their inaugural repast, the creatures began to hack and gash at the diaphanous membranes of their pods. In a frenzy, they struggled deliriously to birth themselves and sate their hunger.

Spurred by the frantic hatching all around him, Jackson tunneled deeper and deeper into the vile mess. Each time the queen tick hammered into the mound, he could feel the weight of the pods flex and shift. But the more he writhed and kicked, the further he got from her increasingly manic attack. When it became clear that her rampage was fruitless, the queen tick ceased her flailing and began to scuttle around to see where her prey could have escaped to.

Chapter 40

IN A EUPHORIC STUPOR, KARL Kellerman watched the queen tick rage, unable to locate Jackson in the mounds of gelatinous eggs on the plant floor. The German exalted in the profane power and malignance of the monster. And when she tilted up and saw him above her, he felt an electric jolt of excitement sizzle through him. In that exquisite moment, the German sensed a malevolent communion binding their souls together.

But he also had a job to do.

Turning again on Emmaline, the now-deranged Kellerman lunged, stabbing the knife forward with wild abandon. Emmaline swiped the empty backpack at the oncoming blade and parried it away, incensing Kellerman even further. He slashed the knife back towards her. This time, in her effort to dodge, Emmaline lost her balance and fell hard onto the platform.

When she scrambled back up to her feet again, Kellerman was right there. Emmaline tried to back away from him, but she couldn't. She was at the end of the platform, back to the massive pesticide tank, with the C4 device mounted just inches away.

2:14

2:13

2:12

"Nowhere left to run, Indian girl!" Kellerman growled.

He cocked the knife back and stabbed down at Emmaline. She caught his wrist with both hands and pushed with all her might to keep the jagged blade from hacking into her.

They struggled like that for a long moment. Emmaline's back pressed against the tank, as Kellerman used the full weight of his body to bring the blade closer and closer to her face.

Emmaline's wildest hope was that she could hold Kellerman off just long enough for the timer to count down to zero. Just long enough to blow them, the queen, and the entire nest to Kingdom Come. But even with just one arm, Kellerman was the stronger of the two. With her arms starting to tremble and give, she realized that the battle was about to end.

Then, from just below them, came another ghastly scream.

Unable to locate Jackson, the monstrous tick had set its sights on the brawling humans above her. Tilting back on her hind legs, the creature thrust upwards, stretched out to her full height, and extended her front legs high into the air. Balanced there, she slashed one of her massive claws out. Though missing her prey, the claw sliced right through the catwalk like a steak knife through tin foil. Too heavy to sustain that posture, the queen crashed back onto the plant floor with a thundering boom.

The violent blow tore away a section of the platform eight feet long and knocked Emmaline and Kellerman free of each other.

Emmaline went tumbling over the side of the catwalk, just managing to hook an arm over the rail and prevent a plunge to the floor below.

Kellerman lost his balance entirely and dropped the knife. When he stepped back to steady himself, his foot found nothing but air—that section of the platform was now gone—and he fell. Desperately, he grabbed for the bottom railing, and with a jerk that popped his shoulder completely out of its socket, he caught himself.

Screaming in pain, he tried to hoist himself up. But the dislocated arm was now worthless, and with neither of his arms functional, it was all he could do just to keep himself suspended above the nest.

Not far away, Emmaline found a footing and hoisted herself back onto the listing scaffold. Once she was securely onto that section of catwalk, she looked down at Kellerman dangling from the severed platform. He glared back at her with terror, hate, and fury all playing in his dull, blanched eyes.

As Emmaline watched, the queen tick lurched up once more from below them. Stretching out to full length she reached for Kellerman, who was oblivious to his impending doom from below. Then, with a bestial shriek, the savage colossus plunged a thick claw into his lower back. crunching through the base of his spine and stabbing out from his stomach.

A thick spew of blood and intestines exploded out of him, along with an agonized howl. His hand released limply from the rail, but the monster held him there like a trophy impaled on her bloody claw.

With one more triumphant screech, the queen let her weight bring her crashing back to the floor on all eights. When she slapped Kellerman into the concrete, his entire body shattered and caved in, blood spattering in all directions. From every direction, famished tick larvae swarmed over him, greedily claiming their first taste of human blood.

From above, Emmaline watched Kellerman meet his pitiful end. But her own immediate peril prevented her from relishing his gruesome comeuppance.

The queen tick's attack had left a gap in the catwalk that was too big for her to leap across, cutting her off from any of the ladders to the plant floor. And the platform she stood on was so twisted and bent that she could no longer reach the C4. She could still see the detonator, though, as it counted inexorably down.

1:24

1:23

1:22

"Jackson!" she cried out, hoping beyond hope that he was still alive and might be able to help.

But as she scanned around the floor of the tank farm below, there was no sign of him. The only things she could see were the raging queen tick and massive piles of dark, muculent eggs.

And then it hit her.

Oh my God, Emmaline, she thought, *you can't!*

She glanced back again at the detonator, the numbers dwindling dangerously down.

1:11

1:10

1:09

When Emmaline turned back around, the queen tick was ranging up once more, determined to eradicate this infestation of troublesome bipeds once and for all. Back up on her hind legs, she thrashed upwards with a front claw.

Emmaline had no choice.

She jumped.

With every bit of strength she could muster, Emmaline leapt off the steel suspension just as the queen tick hammered the platform away.

Plummeting, Emmaline felt her body go clammy and cold. Sickness churned in her stomach, and she became so lightheaded she almost passed out. It was only a few seconds in the air, but the sensation of the fall suspended her senses and sent tremors of overwhelming emotion rippling through her.

And then it was over.

Emmaline crashed down onto a slimy mound of mucus-filled pods, sending geysers of gooey, tawny ooze splashing into the air. The impact of her fall knocked the wind out of her and ruptured, squashed, and splattered countless tick eggs. But there were enough of the oblong jellied pods piled up to soften her landing.

Stunned that she had reached the large mass of eggs that she'd been aiming for, Emmaline heaved and gulped to get her breath back. As she squiggled around trying to get free of the egg muck all around her, the queen tick thumped back to the ground and turned to find her prey.

Spotting Emmaline, the monster tick attacked.

A mighty claw carved through the egg mound just behind a fleeing Emmaline, who swam through the pile in desperation. Egg slime and butchered ticks sprayed in all directions as the queen tick raged. Emmaline rolled and slid off the slick pile as the queen trudged right into the living dune, stomping and trampling even more of her brood.

When Emmaline finally tumbled to solid ground, she looked up to see the queen tick towering right over her. Done with this game, the enraged gargantuan raised a massive claw to finish Emmaline off.

Just before she could strike, the queen issued a ferocious screech. At first, it sounded like an inhuman battle cry. But as it stretched on Emmaline recognized it as something else.

A scream of pain.

Emmaline saw the queen's claw drop to the ground. When she smelled the rancid stench of burning chitin fill the air, she knew what was happening.

A blistering column of yellow and orange flames buffeted the queen tick from behind. Black smoke and fire rose from the beast's hind quarter as she thrashed and pitched and turned away from Emmaline to face this new attack.

At the other end of the torrent of fire was Jackson.

Sitting on the floor propped against one of the tanks, Jackson looked half-dead. Bloody and pale, his hair and clothes were slick and matted with gobs of slime. Every bit of exposed flesh—from his face and neck down to his hands—appeared hideously engraved with gashes and cuts from the hatchling ticks.

But he still held the flamethrower as it spit its blazing wrath towards the queen.

The monster tick turned on him, and Jackson ceased his assault, resting the weapon in his lap. He took deep, rasping breaths, as if struggling to gather enough strength just to raise the weapon again and resume the attack. But when the queen advanced, Jackson did just that, tilting the nozzle towards her to discharge another blaze of fire and fury. This time the flames washed over the monster's front legs and head, engulfing her freakish chelicerae and scalding her mouthparts.

The queen stopped, reeling from the intense attack.

But she didn't retreat.

Once again, Jackson paused the assault, just long enough to cry out to Emmaline.

"Go!" he shouted with as much breath as he could muster.

Emmaline couldn't fathom leaving him there. But even as she took a halting step towards him, she saw his plaintive gaze and stopped. His eyes were filled with pain and desperation…but also determination. And she knew that even if she could get to him and drag him out, Jackson would not last much longer.

"Go," he repeated, quieter but with a steely resolve.

Then he smiled at Emmaline, looked back to the queen, and unleashed one last deluge of fire into her face.

The mutant queen screeched and shrieked but moved forward. Ignoring her burning flesh and boiling innards, she walked straight through the inferno to end the battle.

High above them, the numbers continued to count down.

0:24

0:23

0:22

Though Emmaline couldn't see the detonator, she knew full well that her time was running out.

Spinning around, she raced out of the tank farm and into the main plant, leaping over and running through scampering tick larvae as she went. In seconds she was in the wide hallway and running towards the lobby. Flinging open the heavy door, she slammed into the reception desk, scooted around it, and punched open the front door with the heels of her hands. Once outside, she rushed past the parked ATV and sprinted madly away from the building.

Inside the plant, the queen tick's head and scutum and front legs were covered in flaming gel. She was near delirium from the pain and fury, and her screeching had reached a demented pitch.

But just as Jackson began to swell with hope that he might finish her off, the flamethrower choked and sputtered. With a whimper, it spit out one final dribble of fire. Jackson continued to twitch his finger at the trigger, but the weapon didn't respond.

It was out of fuel.

Jackson dropped his arms limply and let the hose fall into his lap. Defeated, he looked up at his conqueror.

The queen tick—literally ablaze from Jackson's unrelenting assault— bent over him. Her mouthparts blistered and smoldering, she leaned her blackened chelicera towards him, ready to cut him in half.

But she never got the chance.

The booming explosions above them began with one blinding flash as the C4 detonated. The thundering eruption of the first tank followed a split second later. Filled to the brim with highly flammable compounds, the blast from that one enormous container alone might have destroyed the plant. But then—one by one in rapid succession—each of the massive vessels in the tank farm ignited. In seconds, the chain reaction had reached every single tank, tub, and vat of chemicals in the entire complex.

Outside, Emmaline—racing across the front courtyard away from the plant—was buffeted to the ground by the immense force of the blast behind her.

Looking back, she saw the night erupt into a torrid spectacle of fire and billowing smoke. Explosion after explosion sent swelling fireballs higher and higher toward the stars, transforming darkness into day as the raging columns of flame painted the night sky in vivid hues of orange and red.

A chilling chorus of aberrant shrieks rang out with the first explosion, and the hideous ear-splitting screech of the queen tick rose unmistakably above the din. But as quickly as it began, the fiendish score ceased. It was first drowned out by the succession of thundering booms and then silenced entirely as the mammoth conflagration incinerated the demon choir.

With the acrid stink of burning chemicals and scalding tick flesh stinging her nostrils, Emmaline lay on the ground. A hail of debris and ash rained down around her as a sob rose in her throat.

"Goodbye, Jackson," she whispered, unable to look away from the towering inferno that spired high into the night.

She had lost her friend and mentor, but together they had obliterated the mutant tick nest.

Chapter 41

IT WAS TWO WEEKS BEFORE state and federal officials felt confident that they had exterminated the last of the mutant horde. It had required an enormous mobilization of resources, including local law enforcement, Wisconsin National Guard troops, and the deployment of active-duty soldiers up from Fort Riley in Kansas. For a time, Tomahawk Hollow felt like a war zone as military transports and equipment shuttled in and out of town both day and night.

With the queen tick incinerated and most of the adult ticks, hatchlings, and eggs already destroyed, the advanced weaponry of the defense personnel was more than sufficient to get control of the situation. It was just a matter of tracking and hunting down any of the stray arachnids that had fled Tomahawk Hollow or were still roaming through the sewers. Scores of soldiers scoured the forest, dredged the river, and searched every nook and cranny in a thirty-mile radius to ensure that every last mutant beast had been destroyed.

On the night of the tick invasion, it was the State Police and Sheriff Buckley's deputies that had secured the town. They had arrived on the scene expecting to find some sort of brawl or large-scale public disturbance. But once they recovered from the shock of what they actually discovered there, they got to work evacuating survivors and clearing the town of the mutant infestation. All in all, close to three hundred men, women, and children were slaughtered on the night of the Harvest Moon Jubilee. Perhaps a thousand or more were injured or traumatized by the catastrophic horrors they experienced.

The massive explosion on the outskirts of town quickly brought a unit of cops and deputies to the Tomahawk Hollow Pesticides plant. Emmaline met them and convinced them to dispatch a rescue mission into the woods to retrieve Elmer and Dan. But when they tried to evacuate her to a hospital in Antigo, she refused and demanded that they take her into town.

It took her some time to track down Donovan, who was helping coordinate the effort to clear the ticks out of the downtown area. When she found him, she quickly briefed him on Kellerman's threat to Dr. Sokolová. Together they got in touch with a friend of Donovan's at the FBI, who assured them he would take it from there. When a German hit squad infiltrated the Institute of Parasitology several hours later, a team of Czech military police were waiting to apprehend them.

At the end of that crazy night, an exhausted Emmaline was removed to Fort McCoy, an Army Reserve installation in Western Wisconsin. She received medical treatment and was held in isolation, interrupted intermittently by a series of debriefings. Over three weeks, she endured long interviews with officials from the Department of Homeland Security, the Centers for Disease Control and Prevention, the Environmental Protection Agency, and the FBI. Near the end of her detainment, she even spoke with representatives from the World Health Organization and Interpol, which was investigating the involvement of Blutmond Holdings in what was officially being called the "Tomahawk Hollow Incident."

As it turns out, no paper trail could be found connecting Blutmond Holdings to Tomahawk Hollow Pesticides, and a tangled web of shell companies and forged documents obscured its actual ownership.

The German hit team arrested in the Czech Republic revealed under questioning that a man named Karl Kellerman had hired them. But despite their assertions and Emmaline's testimony of his involvement in the matter, there was no evidence of Karl Kellerman's actual existence.

The room at the Main Street Inn where the nuclear device had been recovered was registered to a John Smith, who had also rented a house on the outskirts of town. Beyond the suitcase bomb, though, no weapons or equipment had been left behind at either location. Remarkably, both locations were entirely devoid of fingerprints or identifying DNA of any kind…including any belonging to the cleaning staff, previous guests, or the owners themselves.

For her part, Emmaline steadfastly insisted that the black van parked outside Tomahawk Hollow Pesticides when she and Jackson arrived there was gone when she later fled the building. She returned to this issue repeatedly in her various debriefings, emphasizing in particular the egg they had found in the van. However, the official report indicated that the van and anything inside it had been incinerated in the massive plant explosion.

Almost a month after her detainment began, Emmaline was unceremoniously released. A reservist in camouflage fatigues loaded her into a military jeep, drove her across the state, thanked her, and dropped her off in front of the Tomahawk Hollow Gazette.

Inside, Emmaline found the office a mere shell of itself. The computers, cameras, recorders, storage devices, and files had all been seized, creating an eerie sense of emptiness and finality.

Walking over to her desk, Emmaline spun her office chair around a few times and then flopped down into it. She leaned back, closed her eyes, and tried to hold back tears. She had cried enough over the past month, she decided.

"Hey."

Emmaline snapped around and saw Donovan standing in the doorway.

"I asked them to give me a heads-up when they were planning to send you back," Donovan explained. "Are you okay?"

She shrugged. "I guess so."

Donovan looked around the empty office and shook his head.

"All that," he noted wryly, "and you didn't even get the story."

Emmaline was well aware of it. One of the biggest news events ever, and every journalist in the world except her had the chance to report it.

"What did it look like?"

"The coverage?" Donovan asked. "It was crazy for a while. Cameras and reporters everywhere. And then something happened somewhere else, and they all moved on."

Emmaline laughed. "I guess that's how the news works these days."

"Yeah, well, I wouldn't go on social media any time soon if I were you," Donovan warned. "It turns out that half the country thinks we're scammers and con artists, and most of the rest think we're a bunch of kooks. Apparently, we've all been doxed, whatever the hell that means."

Shaking her head, Emmaline sighed. She might have known.

"I can't stay," Donovan apologized, "but I just wanted to check in."

"Thanks," Emmaline smiled.

"But…" Donovan hesitated a moment.

"What?"

"Do you want to grab a bite to eat tonight, maybe?"

Emmaline felt a swell in her chest, and the tears that almost came earlier threatened again to roll down her cheeks. But she swallowed hard and stopped them.

"I do," she said, clearing her throat, "but not tonight, okay? I feel like I need to get my legs under me."

Embarrassed, Donovan nodded and began to turn back to the door.

"Tim," she said quickly, turning him hesitantly back around. "I really do. Soon."

When Donovan looked at her again she was smiling warmly. He smiled back and nodded.

"Well, what are you going to do now?" he asked. "Get the paper up and running again?"

"I don't think so," Emmaline sighed again. "This was Jackson's, and I think he and the Gazette deserve to be remembered for everything they meant to Tomahawk Hollow."

Donovan nodded. "Where does that leave you, then?"

"I was actually thinking maybe I'd write a book," Emmaline smiled.

"A book?" Donovan laughed, "That's so…*old media*."

Emmaline shrugged.

"Well, I think that's a great idea," Donovan continued. "Besides, I hear that *you people* are supposed to be pretty good storytellers."

This time Emmaline laughed. "*Us people*, right."

"So, a novel?"

"Nah," Emmaline shook her head. "I'm a journalist. And, besides, you know what they say…"

"No, what do they say?"

Emmaline shrugged again. "Truth is always stranger than fiction."

Chapter 42

ELMER DOBBS WAITED ON THE porch.

He was still limited by a full leg cast and had left his crutches in the truck. As a result, it was a real struggle to hop and pull his way up the front steps without dropping the offering he carried in his arms. Then, after all that, he had debated whether to even ring the doorbell at all. But having come this far and dreading the journey back down the steps, he had gone ahead and pressed the bell. Now he just wanted to turn and run, but with that damn cast he knew he wouldn't get far.

Even as he debated his escape options, though, Olive Butler opened the front door with a welcoming smile.

It had been well over a month since Elmer had seen Dan or Olive. He had attended Cheri Butler's funeral in early October, and the Butler's had attended services for his boy Dave just a week later. Funerals in Tomahawk Hollow were small affairs in those days, with so many families grieving and burying their own. But considering that their kids had died together, Elmer and the Butlers felt strongly about supporting each other.

"Elmer!" Olive beamed and then choked back a tear. Finally, she wrapped him in a warm hug. "We're so happy you came."

Elmer hooked an arm halfway around her and gave an awkward squeeze. Then he stiffened up again and pulled away. Olive released him and stepped back herself.

"And you brought a pie!" she exclaimed as if the plate were piled high with Gold, Frankincense, and Myrrh.

"I didn't bake it or nuthin'," Elmer said, holding the pie out for her. "I just ordered it from Gail's." Then, remembering his manners, he added quickly, "Happy Thanksgiving."

"Happy Thanksgiving, Elmer!" she smiled, taking the pie. "Come in! Dan's just finishing up in the kitchen."

"Course he is," Elmer muttered, shaking his head. With the screen door still propped open, he remained half in, half out of the house.

"Elmer, Happy Thanksgiving." Dan joined them, wiping his hands on his long turkey-decorated apron before shaking Elmer's hand.

"Nice dress, Martha," Elmer said, but still squeezed Dan's hand when they shook. "Thanks for invitin' me."

Olive excused herself and whisked the pie away into the kitchen, leaving Dan and Elmer standing in the open doorway.

"We're happy you came, Elmer," Dan smiled once they were alone. "How've you been doing?" His voice cracked just a bit with the question, but Elmer didn't call him on it.

"I been doin' okay," he answered softly. "But the house is awful quiet."

"I know. But you're welcome here any time. You know that, right?"

Elmer's face flushed warm, and he felt a dampness fill the corner of his eye. Dan patted his arm but had the decency to turn around and start back towards the kitchen before the tear rolled down Elmer's cheek.

"Can I get you a beer?" Dan called back.

Elmer wiped it away and limped into the house.

"'Bout time you offered," he answered, letting the door swing shut behind him.

THE END

THANK YOU FOR VISITING TICK TOWN!

Please leave a rating and review to let me know what you think!

I hope that you enjoyed reading it as much as I enjoyed writing it. Despite all the blood, sweat, and tears that go into producing a book, it's all just words on a page until someone picks it up and reads it. So thank you for helping me bring my work to life by taking the time to read it.

Please subscribe to my mailing list for giveaways and exclusive stories, as well as updates on events and future books…some of which are right around the corner! subscribepage.io/christophermicklos

And join my social media community by following me on any or all of these platforms:

Facebook facebook.com/ChristopherAMicklos

Instagram instagram.com/christophermicklos

Bluesky @horrorwriterchris.bsky.social

X @chrismicklos

Website christophermicklos.com

CASTLE BRIDGE MEDIA RECOMMENDS...

If you liked this book, you might also enjoy reading the following titles from Castle Bridge Media available on Amazon or by order at your favorite book store:

The 23rd Hero
By Rebecca Anne Nguyen

ANIMAL CHARMER
By Rain Nox
Animal Charmer
Magic & Melody

Austinites
By In Churl Yo

Bloodsucker City
By Jim Towns

SOUL CATCHER
By Don Sawyer
The Burning Gem
The Tunnels of Buda

THE CASTLE OF HORROR ANTHOLOGY SERIES
Volume 1
Volume 2: Holiday Horrors
Volume 3: Scary Summer
 Stories
Volume 4: Women Running
 From Houses
Volume 5: Thinly Veiled:
 The 70s
Volume 6: Femme Fatales*
Volume 7: Love Gone Wrong
Volume 8: Thinly Veiled:
 The 80s
Volume 9: Young Adult
Volume 10: Thinly Veiled:
 Saturday Mournings
Volume 11: Revenge
Volume 12: Ripped From
 The Headlines
Edited By Jason Henderson
and In Churl Yo
*Edited By P.J. Hoover

Child of Dark Water
By E..G. Rand

Castle of Horror Podcast Book of Great Horror: Our Favorites, Top Tens and Bizarre Pleasures
Edited By Jason Henderson

Cherry Dark
By R.L. Wilburn

Dream State
By Martin Ott

Dominic
By Lee Guzman

FRENCH DECEPTION
By Janice Nagourney
A Forgery in Paris
A Forgery in Lyon
A Forgery in Marseille

FuturePast Sci-Fi Anthology
Edited by In Churl Yo

GLAZIER'S GAP
Ghosts of the Forbidden
By Leanna Renee Hieber

Hellfall
By Jay Gould

Isonation
By In Churl Yo

JAYU CITY CHRONICLES
By Chris M. Arnone
The Hermes Protocol
Necropolis Alpha

Junk Film: Why Bad Movies Matter
By Katharine Coldiron

MID-LIFE CRISIS THRILLERS
18 Miles From Town
By Jason Henderson
Lost Angel
By Sam Knight
Ties That Kill
By Deven Greene

Nightwalkers: Gothic Horror Movies
By Bruce Lanier Wright

THE PATH
By David Bowles
The Blue-Spangled Blue
The Deepest Green

SURF MYSTIC
By Peyton Douglas
Night of the Book Man
Dark of the Curl

The Thing That Happened When We Were Little
By Caroline Kelly Franklin

Tick Town
By Christopher A. Micklos

Yesterday's Tomorrows: The Golden Age of Science Fiction Movies
By Bruce Lanier Wright

Please remember to leave us your reviews on Amazon and Goodreads!

THANK YOU FOR SUPPORTING INDEPENDENT PUBLISHERS AND AUTHORS!
castlebridgemedia.com